The GRUMP who saved CHRISTMAS

T.K. LEIGH WRITING AS

TRACY LEIGH

THE GRUMP WHO SAVED CHRISTMAS

Published by Carpe Per Diem Publishing, Inc

Cover Design: Cat Head Media, Inc.

Cover assets used under license from Deposit Photo

For a full list of all of Tracy's books, including recommended reading order, please visit her website:

www.tracyleigh.com

Books and reading order for her spicy billionaire romance alter ego, T.K. Leigh, can be found here:

www.tkleighauthor.com

For exclusive sales and excerpts,
sign up for Tracy Leigh's VIP list!

https://www.tracyleighbooks.com/subscribe

Or scan the code below

To everyone who prefers some spice in their Christmas novels.
This one's for you…

ONE

Parker

"Is there nothing I can do, Max? Maybe talk to someone higher up at the bank and explain the situation? See if they're willing to give me a little longer to pay?"

The local diner is alive with the chatter of patrons and forks scraping against plates. My accountant avoids my eyes as he silently arranges the papers in front of him, probably to delay telling me we've already done everything we can.

When Max called over the weekend and asked me to meet him for breakfast today, I should have known it was to deliver bad news. Over the past several years that he's handled my financials, he's never offered to buy me breakfast if he has good news. Pretty sure this is his way of softening the blow, more or less.

So sorry you're about to lose everything you and your parents worked hard to accomplish, but here's a delicious Belgium waffle topped with chocolate syrup and whipped cream to make it hurt less.

While it does take the sting out a little — chocolate always does — nothing can make the reality of my current situation any easier to swallow.

I have one month to come up with my overdue mortgage and property taxes or the bank will initiate foreclosure proceedings.

Merry fucking Christmas to me.

"I wish there was, Parker," Max replies with all the sympathy I've come to expect from the older gentleman.

"What about someone investing in the tax lien? You told me that was a thing."

"And it is, but typically for smaller amounts. You're looking at a tax default of nearly a hundred grand."

"It's thirty acres," I argue in my defense.

"Most investors aren't interested in offering a tax lien for that much. Not when there's a risk they may not be able to collect on the lien."

"We've seen higher numbers this past weekend than we have over the last few years. We don't even have all the decorations up yet. Which means the next several weeks will be even busier, especially with the tree lighting ceremony and the Christmas festival opening. You know how busy we get. People travel from all over to come to Christmas at Holley Ridge."

"I'm aware. But with your current bookings and projections, can you really expect to make a hundred grand above and beyond your overhead? That doesn't even take into account the amount you're in default on your mortgage."

"It could happen," I say, although my voice lacks even a modicum of conviction.

While this may be the busiest time of the year for my event space and quaint inn set on a beautiful lake, it's also my most costly with all the extras I plan for the holiday season. Some would consider it excessive, but my parents loved decorating Holley Ridge for Christmas. Loved welcoming hundreds of people from all over onto their property to celebrate the season.

I hate the idea that everything they worked hard for is about to go up in flames.

"Have you given any more thought to the offer you received before Thanksgiving? It's more than fair."

"I already told you. I'm not interested in selling."

Max pushes out a long breath laden with frustration. "Parker, you may not have a choice. I get that Holley Ridge has a special meaning to you, and unfortunately, you got hit with hard times almost immediately after you finished the construction of the inn and restoration of the barn. If the world hadn't shut down and both the tourism and wedding industry hadn't taken as big of a hit as they did in the months to follow, we probably wouldn't be sitting here right now. The banks were willing to work with you in the beginning, but now…"

"I know, Max. I just…" I shake my head, my throat closing up. "I promised my dad I'd take care of Holley Ridge. I can't give up. Not without a fight." I slide out of the booth, tugging on my coat and slinging my purse over my shoulder. "When does the bank need the money?"

"January second. If it's not received by the end of the day, they'll be filing a notice of foreclosure with the clerk of court the following morning."

"I'll have it," I tell Max with all the confidence I can muster, not allowing a single shred of doubt to creep in. Then I spin around and make my way out of the diner, pretending nothing is wrong. That I'm not on the brink of losing everything my parents worked hard for.

That *I've* worked hard for.

I emerge onto the sidewalk of historic downtown

Sycamore Falls and wave at several locals as they pass, smiling when they tell me how much they're looking forward to the tree lighting ceremony this weekend. I don't let them see my unease over the prospect that it may be the last tree lighting ceremony I ever host.

Holley Ridge has been in my family for generations and was once a working ranch. Over the years, the focus shifted from raising livestock to breeding, training, and boarding horses. Now, the property is used to host events in the barn I spent most of my inheritance restoring several years ago. But what it's most well-known for is being the home of the Holley Ridge Christmas Festival.

What started as my parents going all out to decorate their property for the holidays eventually grew into an annual tradition, each year's decorations and festivities bigger than the last. Now, the festival boasts a market filled with vendors selling various gift items, an ice-skating rink, horse-drawn carriage rides, and even a polar express "train" to see Santa.

My heart squeezes at the notion of this all going away. Of never being able to witness the joy that fills a child's face as they meet Santa for the first time. Of not watching families make ornaments together that they'll hang on their tree for years to come. Of not watching couples snuggle up on a horse-drawn carriage as they share a special moment.

Leaving downtown Sycamore Falls behind me, I follow a dirt path through towering trees and onto Holley Ridge, the farmhouse-style inn soon coming into view. The white siding and dark wood trim contrasts with the deep green wreaths looped across the door and windows, a few of my employees standing on ladders, hanging white lights along the roof.

I continue past the inn, admiring the stunning view of snowcapped mountains reflecting in the lake along with the towering Norway spruce that's served as the centerpiece of the annual Holley Ridge Christmas Festival longer than I've been alive.

I follow the sound of hammers hitting nails and find the Sycamore Falls Fire Department hard at work building the North Pole area where kids will soon be able to meet Santa. A lump forms in my throat over the idea that this may be the last year I'll be able to watch this amazing transformation. But I can't think like that. I *will* find a way to save this place.

Pushing out a long sigh, I turn from the lakeside path and climb onto the back veranda of the inn, slipping into the high-ceilinged lobby. The instant I do, I'm meet with warmth.

And an older woman perched on a stool in the lobby lounge, a pair of binoculars pressed to her face.

"Are you bird watching again?" I ask as I sidle up to Grandma Estelle.

While she's not technically anyone's grandma — she has no family to speak of and never married — most locals call her Grandma Estelle, especially at Holley Ridge. She worked here when this was still a working ranch, teaching young kids how to ride horses. Hell, she taught *me* how to ride. Now, she helps at the inn doing whatever I need her to.

"I thought they all flew south for the winter."

"Not bird watching, Parker. Man watching." Her eyes crinkle from behind the binoculars, her lips curving into a devious grin. "Would you look at those muscles. I bet he's got a great ass. God bless the Sycamore Falls Fire Department."

"Estelle!" I exclaim, glancing around to make sure no guests are near enough to overhear.

"Speaking of great asses…," she continues, not looking away from her binoculars. "There's someone here to see you. A rather attractive male with what appears to be a great behind."

"Who?"

"Don't know."

"What does he want?"

"Don't know," she repeats.

"Where is he? Or do you not know that, either?"

"That I do know. He's in your office. He'll be the one in the suit that looks like it was tailor made to his sexy bod."

I roll my eyes. "If this is yet another attempt to get me to date, I'm not interested."

"I had nothing to do with this, Parker darling. He just showed up and asked for you. I told him you weren't here, but he insisted he'd wait."

I pinch the bridge of my nose, fighting back a tension headache. No doubt it's probably someone from the bank to discuss my outstanding loan. Max warned they may pay me a visit.

"Thanks, Estelle."

"Hot, damn, he bent over," she remarks excitedly. "Those boys really need to put together a calendar."

"I couldn't agree more," I murmur as I head toward my office, jazz-inspired Christmas music filling the air, lending to the festive atmosphere in the beautifully decorated lobby.

After stopping by the front desk to make sure everything's running smoothly, I turn down the administrative wing and step into my office. A man stands by the window, studying the construction of the festival with a confused expression.

Like Estelle said, he's dressed in a smooth, black suit, the lines of it accentuating every contour of his built physique, his pants falling perfectly from his hips. The sprinkle of stubble along his jawline only adds to the effect, making me wonder what it would feel like to have his face buried between my legs, scratching against my thighs.

There's no two ways about it. This man is the epitome of suit porn. The type of guy I picture in my mind whenever reading yet another one of the romance novels Estelle insists I read so she has someone to talk to about it.

"Excuse me, ma'am."

His deep voice cuts through my fantasies about having his mouth on me. That's what a dry spell can do to a girl.

I dart my head up, the heat in his stare causing a shiver to trickle through me.

"Y-yes," I finally answer, pretending his mere proximity doesn't have my heart skipping a beat or my stomach fluttering.

"I'm looking for Parker Holley. I was hoping to speak with him about an urgent matter."

I unbutton my coat and hang it on the rack. "You *are* speaking with *her*."

His eyes widen. Obviously, this guy assumed I was male. With a name like Parker, I get that a lot, especially in the business world. In my experience, most people assume I'd *have* to have a pair of hairy testicles and a penis to run a business.

Fucking patriarchal society.

"My apologies, ma'am."

His full lips curve into a sinful smile, his brown eyes sparkling as they rake over me. Then he extends his hand and we shake, my skin heating from the feel of his big, rough hand on me. If I knew a bank employee was this attractive, I would have defaulted on my loan a long time ago.

"My name's Callum Reed. I'm hoping to discuss the offer my firm made on this property."

And like that, all his attractiveness disappears.

TWO

Callum

I lay on the charm as I stare into Parker Holley's brilliant blue eyes, still somewhat surprised by how young she is.

And how *female* she is.

It hadn't even crossed my mind that she'd be… well, a she. I simply assumed she was some middle-aged man, as is often the case in these types of situations.

I've been in the real estate development business for over a decade now. Normally, we deal with older people clinging onto their property in the hopes of a miracle, allowing them to suddenly be able to afford the land they haven't been able to pay the mortgage or taxes on for quite some time.

Actually, that's not entirely true.

My *business partner* deals with the people we're trying to buy property from.

I prefer to scope out potential properties and run the numbers on what kind of risk versus reward we're looking at if we procure it. Crunching numbers and analyzing data is my forte, not socializing or engaging in small talk with someone trying to hold onto some rundown land that's been in their family for generations. Daniel has always been much better with that side of our business, which is why we make such a great team.

But this property has been on my radar for a while, especially with its location near a popular skiing and recreation area within a short drive of Reno. My firm can make millions off building luxury timeshares on this thirty-acre parcel of land.

I didn't expect the only person standing between me and adding several zeros to my bank account to be a young blonde who has snowmen dangling from her ears and is wearing a t-shirt that says "Let's get elfed up".

And I certainly didn't expect her to be absolutely gorgeous.

Blonde hair as smooth as corn silk. Long legs that seem to go on for miles. And don't even get me started on those lips, full and painted a bright red that makes being surrounded by all this unnecessary Christmas cheer slightly more bearable.

Until she rips her hand from mine, her mouth turning into a scowl, her eyes narrowing in anger.

"Get. Out. If I'd been even remotely interested in your firm's offer, I would have had my attorney reach out to you. Apparently, you can't take a hint." She crosses her arms, drawing my attention to her full chest. "This property isn't for sale."

"It may not be for sale yet, but based on my research, you're in debt up to your eyeballs. It's my understanding the bank will be moving to foreclose on the property in the beginning of the year unless you can come up with the amount you owe on back taxes and the mortgage you defaulted on, which totals over a half-million dollars. Trust me, Ms. Holley. If you let this go to foreclosure, you won't get remotely close to what I'm offering. If I were you, I'd give this serious consideration."

I reach into my commuter bag and retrieve another copy of the same offer I sent several weeks ago.

"I don't care what you're offering." She pinches her lips into a tight line, refusing to even look at the papers in my hand. "I'm not interested in selling to some real estate development firm that's going to gut this place and turn it into timeshares with no personality. People come to Sycamore Falls because it hasn't been commercialized like so many of the other communities in the area. It's one of the last true mountain basin small towns, and I'll do whatever is necessary in order to keep it that way."

"I appreciate your...affection for your hometown, but the small businesses here would see a huge boost if I were to develop luxury vacation homes. It could inject millions in tourism dollars into the community. It's a win-win for all involved, especially for you. The numbers don't lie, Ms. Holley. You're hemorrhaging money. And all this Christmas frivolity isn't helping."

"Of course it is!" She throws up her hands in exasperation. "People come here year after year to experience Christmas at Holley Ridge. If you did even a modicum of research on this property, you would have learned it's been an annual tradition around here for over forty years. People travel hundreds of miles for this."

"But look at all the money you waste on it. Money you don't get back, especially since you forego hosting weddings between Thanksgiving and the new year. Free hot chocolate. That ice skating rink must cost a bit to maintain." I gesture out the window at a temporary ice skating rink near a towering Christmas tree. "And how about the sleigh rides I saw being advertised? It's my understanding this property no longer boards horses. It must cost you a small fortune to use those horses and the sleigh every night, not to mention pay whoever's manning it."

"Again, Mr. Reed. It all adds to the magic and wonder of the holiday season. Plus, the owner of the farm where the horses and carriage come from cuts me a deal because he supports the Holley Ridge Christmas Festival. Just like everyone else in this town."

"But not enough to allow you the use of his horses and carriage for free?" I arch a brow.

"He deserves to be paid for his time and services."

"Don't you think you do, too? All of this ridiculousness…" I wave my hand at nothing in particular, everything excessive with an overabundance of Christmas cheer. "It's making you lose money. There's no profit in any of it."

"Maybe not on a line item, but some of our loyal customers have come to expect certain things over the years. I'm happy to give them a place to slow down and spend time with their families."

"Nobody wants to spend time with their families," I scoff, rolling my eyes at the ridiculousness of the idea that kids these days would willingly sit in a car for hours just to have their photo taken with a fake Santa or stroll through a row of booths containing cheesy Christmas trinkets. They'd much rather stay home and play video games. Or watch TV. Not endure a day filled with forced holiday cheer just to snap a few social media-worthy photos that make them look like a happy family when nothing could be further from the truth.

"If that's what you think, then I feel sorry for you." She places her hands on her hips, her mouth turned into a determined line. "Now if you don't mind, I have an inn to run and a wasteful Christmas season to plan."

I part my lips to renew my argument yet again, but she holds up a hand, cutting me off.

"Don't waste your breath, Mr. Reed. I'm not selling."

"Do you have over a half-million dollars stashed away I don't know about? Maybe in one of the stockings I saw hanging from the chimney with care?" I ask mockingly.

"I don't, but that doesn't matter." She holds her head high, nothing but raw determination filling her expression. "I manifested a solution. Put good energy out into the universe."

I'm not sure what I expected her to say, but it wasn't this.

Since I started in the real estate industry, first by flipping houses, then trying my hand at commercial real estate development in the hopes of making millions, I've dealt with my fair share of sellers who've been reluctant to part with a piece of property, regardless of their inability to afford it any longer. I don't recall a single one of them saying anything remotely like this. Most people, even those less than eager to sell, are realistic about the numbers. They know if they want to have anything to pass down to their kids, they need to accept my offer.

This woman is anything but realistic.

"Manifested a solution?" I repeat, not entirely sure what that means.

"I put it out into the universe that I need a solution, so I'm sure the universe will answer my call."

The furrow in my brow deepens. "And because you put it out into the universe, you think it will just… happen?" I can't hide the skepticism in my voice. I've never heard anything so absurd.

This is why Daniel should be here. He knows how to charm people. Hell, he probably would have helped her manifest good vibes.

"That's what manifesting is. I'm manifesting only good things." Her lips turn down into a scowl, the vein in her forehead pulsing.

I shouldn't find it as attractive as I do, but my god, there's something incredibly appealing about the way she looks at me with pure distaste.

"And you're putting a serious damper on the positive energy and growth mindset I'm trying to maintain. Enough of your bad juju and negative energy." She closes her eyes, pinching her forefinger and thumb together on each hand, as if meditating. "You may leave."

I stare at her for several long moments, feeling like I'm in the middle of a cruel joke. Or a dream.

How can anyone think that as long as you manifest something, it'll happen? Life doesn't work that way. If you want something, you have to work for it. No amount of manifestation or positive energy matters. All that does is hard work and perseverance.

"Leave," she repeats after several moments, her eyes still closed.

I set my jaw, wracking my brain for something I can say to get this woman to listen to reason.

I thought this would be a walk in the park, especially considering the massive debt she currently owes.

Apparently, that doesn't matter to her.

"I'll leave my latest offer with you in case you misplaced the last one." I set it onto her desk. "I look forward to receiving your counter, Ms. Holley."

She doesn't respond, keeping her eyes closed as she murmurs what sounds like daily affirmations.

As I slip out of the office and hear her sing the unmistakable melody to "You're a Mean One Mr. Grinch", followed by the sound of the shredder, I can't help but chuckle.

One thing is certain. Parker Holley is one of the

most intriguing women I've met in quite some time, even if slightly infuriating.

But I won't let her get to me. My firm could make millions on this deal.

And I'm not going to let her stand in my way.

THREE

Callum

The second I step off the elevator and into the reception area of my office in the Financial District of San Francisco, I'm immediately assaulted with a barrage of holiday cheer. I've only been gone twenty-four hours. Yet, in that time, the entire floor has transformed into something straight out of a greeting card, lights and garland strung from every surface, a tree with fake presents placed below it.

Normally, I hate walking into the office this time of year — every day the decorations become more numerous while employees work less.

Now, as I make my way through the office, Christmas music playing at low levels from various workspaces, all I can think about is Parker Holley.

Then again, I haven't stopped thinking about her since she kicked me out of her office yesterday morning. She seemed so certain it would all work out. That the universe will give her what she needs simply because she put good energy out into the world.

Who does that? Who thinks all you have to do is put something out into the universe and it will happen? It's absurd. And goes against every single principle I hold dear.

Regardless, I can't stop thinking about her spirit. Her determination. Her tenacity.

And her lips.

I've definitely spent an unhealthy amount of time thinking about her lips, especially when I was alone in the shower, imagining having her on her knees in front of me with those red lips wrapped around my dick.

Maybe I need to manifest that.

"Good morning, Mr. Reed." My assistant jumps up from her desk the second she sees me.

I scowl when I notice her workspace is now decorated with lights and garland. Not simply because I hate everything Christmas brings to mind. Instead, it's because it reminds me of Parker when I shouldn't be thinking about her in any capacity other than figuring out how to convince her to sell.

"How did it go in Sycamore Falls?" Dakota asks, following me into my office. "It's a shame Holley

Ridge is having so much trouble. I remember my parents taking me there every year to see Santa and make Christmas ornaments."

"Sounds utterly delightful," I reply without a single hint of enthusiasm.

"Just because you have absolutely no Christmas spirit doesn't mean I have to be a Grinch, too," she retorts.

Any of my previous assistants would never speak back to me like this. Not Dakota, though. She's the only one with a strong enough backbone to stand up to me and not take my shit. It's probably why Daniel assigned her to me.

And ensures she's well compensated.

"The owner should have paid her bills. Then you could have continued to waste hours in a car just to get your picture taken with a fake Santa who probably smells like cigarettes and moldy cheese."

"You weren't there when the Christmas festival was open, though. Or when it was all lit up. If you go back then, you'll change your mind." She pauses. "Or maybe not, considering you hate anything that might bring someone joy." She rolls her eyes. "Your schedule today is fairly light. You have a conference call about the Tidewater project this afternoon at one. I already pulled the latest status reports for your review."

"I'll take a look at it." I lower myself onto my

chair and boot up my laptop. "Can you get Daniel on the line for me?"

"He's on his honeymoon," she reminds me.

"So?"

She glowers at me for several moments. "Only you would think it's okay to disturb someone on their honeymoon. I'll try him but I'm not going to hound him if he decides not to answer. Anything else?"

"No. Thank you, Dakota."

She gives me a curt nod, then makes her way out of my office, closing the door behind her. Not surprisingly, a few seconds later, Dakota's voice comes over the speaker, telling me she has Daniel holding.

I grab the receiver and lean back in my chair, looking out the windows of my thirty-seventh floor office, barely able to see much of the city through the thick blanket of fog that seems to permanently settle on San Francisco this time of year.

"You wouldn't disturb me on my honeymoon unless it were important, so I'm guessing yesterday either went quite well and we're about to be hundreds of millions of dollars richer. Or it went horribly and you're calling for advice or to convince me to come home early, in which case I'd say I'm not surprised but I'm not cutting my honeymoon short because you suck at dealing with people."

"Hello to you, too," I reply to Daniel's tirade.

"I'm right, though. Aren't I? It didn't go as you hoped?"

I part my lips, about to tell him just how horribly it went and insist he come home early because this is too important of a deal to lose out on.

Daniel's the salesman between the two of us. I've often said he could sell a glass of water to a drowning man. He has a way of charming people into giving him what he wants.

Not me. I've always been more reserved. More analytical. I love numbers. Love looking at data and predicting an outcome based on facts and statistics. It's safe. Predictable. Certain.

I hate the idea of leaving anything to chance. Of not having complete control.

"Do you ever put something out into the universe in the hopes it's listening and will grant your wish or whatever?" I ask, my question leaving my mouth before I can stop it.

"Like manifestation?"

"Sure. Whatever," I respond somewhat dismissively, not wanting him to think I've spent any time researching manifestation. Or reading books about it. Because I absolutely did nothing like that at all last night, despite what my eBook purchase and internet search history may indicate.

"Hannah's a pretty strong believer in it," he says, referring to his wife. "Negative thoughts attract negative energy. So positive thoughts will attract positive energy."

I nod, having learned quite a bit about the law of attraction last night, regardless of whether I'm willing to admit it. Or actually believe any of it.

Although, for a split second, I wonder if that could be the reason for all the horrible shit I've endured in my life. That my negative outlook may have caused it all.

But I quickly brush it off.

"Do you really think that makes any difference?"

"Where is this coming from?"

"This woman…" I push out an aggravated breath, rubbing my temples. "Parker Holley." Her name comes out with a growl. Still, I can't ignore the warmth filling me from her name on my lips.

"She refused to look at the reality that her property will go to auction if she can't come up with the money she owes. And there's no realistic chance she'll be able to do that in the next four weeks. Instead, she kept going on about putting positive vibes out into the universe as a reason for refusing my offer."

"And you're sure it had nothing to do with your charming personality?" Daniel deadpans.

"I was just being practical. She wouldn't even listen to what I had to say about all the money she was wasting on the Christmas festival."

"So, let me get this straight. You went to see her in

the hopes of getting her to sell us this piece of property that could potentially make us upwards of nine figures, then proceeded to insult her business practices?"

"I simply pointed out that she's not making wise decisions. That she doesn't just need a life preserver but an entire lifeboat. We're offering her precisely that."

Daniel releases a long sigh. "The problem is you only see black and white, Callum. It's how you've always been."

"There only *is* black and white here. She *will* lose her property in January."

"You look at the numbers and think it's impossible for her to come up with the funds she needs to keep her property. This isn't a simple equation for her. Not when she's still hoping for a miracle. This is more than just numbers to her, Cal. It's personal."

"I'm trying to buy a piece of property she owns. It's *always* personal."

"But sometimes it's more personal. Like here. You did your research when coming up with the initial offer. You know this property has been in her family for generations. It's going to take more than just showing up with a distant attitude and spreadsheets of numbers for her to warm up to the idea of selling."

"Maybe you should come home from your honeymoon early so you can handle this," I remark, half joking. Half serious.

"Not a chance in hell." He barks out a laugh. "You're a big boy. You can handle it. But you'll need to change tactics."

"How do you suggest I do that?"

"Since it's personal to her, you need to, dare I say it, get to know her as a person. Not a faceless name who owns a piece of property. You look at all those acres and see dollar signs. Or the amount of debt she owes. She looks at it and sees all the memories it holds."

"That still doesn't change the fact that she can't pay her taxes or her mortgage. That's what I need her to see."

"That's the last thing you need her to see. There's a psychological aspect to convincing someone to part with their property you need to take into account here. In my experience, people are much more likely to cooperate if the buyer is sympathetic to their plight."

"I don't see what difference that will make. It still won't make over a half-million dollars magically appear in her bank account."

"If you want this piece of land, you need to act like someone who gives a shit. And you can't do that by sitting in your office several hundred miles away. You need to be on the front lines. Immerse yourself in her life. Understand why she does what she does. Fair warning, though. You may just have to act like a human being and be friendly. Hold a regular conversation. And if that still doesn't work, I'll be back in a little over two weeks to smooth things over."

"This is becoming much more difficult than I thought it would be," I groan.

"I thought you loved a challenge," Daniel throws back at me.

"I've never backed down from one before. And I have no intention of backing down from this one, either."

"Good. Just do me one favor."

"What's that?"

"Try to act like less of a grumpy old man around this woman, especially if you want her to like you."

"*Like* me?" I scoff dismissively. "What does that have to do with anything?"

"She's not going to sell to someone she doesn't like."

"Fine," I grind out through a tight jaw. "I'll endeavor to be on my best behavior."

"This ought to be good," he mumbles. "Keep me posted."

"Will do."

After we say our goodbyes, I relax into my chair, trying to ignore the sudden fluttering in my chest. I refuse to consider it has anything to do with the prospect of seeing Parker Holley again, blaming it on an internal arrhythmia instead.

I'd rather admit to having heart issues than actually feel something for another woman.

I learned that lesson the hard way years ago. I refuse to make the same mistake again. Not with millions of dollars on the line. I can't afford to lose focus now.

And I refuse to lose focus because of a woman as infuriating as Parker Holley.

FOUR

Parker

"Are you ever going to tell me about the handsome man in a suit from the other day?" Grandma Estelle asks as I wrap garland around one of the columns abutting the archway leading into the formal sitting room of the lobby.

A few guests sit by the fire and take in the transformation this place has made over the past few days. Oversized German glass ornaments hang from the beams of the high ceiling. Poinsettias adorn the coffee table and side tables. To complete the look, mistletoe dangles from every single doorway.

It may be cheesy, but I love this time of year.

So do all the guests who stay here in order to fully immerse themselves in the season.

"There's nothing to tell," I insist, keeping my eyes focused on the task at hand, if for no other reason than to push down the blush building on my cheeks from the mere thought of Callum Reed.

Since his visit, I've thought about those deep, penetrating eyes, sinful mouth, and unshaven jawline more times than I care to admit.

Just because he wore a suit so well it should be illegal doesn't matter. Callum Reed is still a prick. An egotistical, pompous, man-splaining prick who thinks all he has to do is show me the numbers on this property and I'll agree to sell.

Stupid ass.

He probably assumed that just because I'm a woman, I'll go along with whatever he tells me. Maybe even thank him for making me realize how much money I owe.

I know the numbers.

Know how much I owe.

Know the projections.

Know the outlook on the travel and wedding industry.

I live and breathe this stuff day-in and day-out. I'm not some dumb blonde who's running an inn and event facility because it sounds like something fun to do while I wait for a husband to magically appear on my doorstep.

I'm invested in this property. I spent most of my

younger years watching my parents transform it from a horse boarding facility to something magical at Christmas time. When they were gone, I used every penny of my inheritance and the life insurance money to restore the barn into an event space and build an inn, like they often dreamed of doing during their lifetime.

There's no way I'm going to sell to someone who will destroy everything I've built over the years. Everything my parents built. It's too important.

"Just someone who wants to buy Holley Ridge," I tell Estelle. "Owns a real estate development firm that wants to build a bunch of luxury timeshares on the property, considering this is one of the last small towns that hasn't been completely commercialized for all the snow bunnies. Too much of this area has been developed, and not in a good way. I won't let some real estate development firm come in and destroy this place, too. Not until I have no other choice."

"And how close are you getting to that point?" Estelle asks somewhat hesitantly.

I exhale, my throat becoming tight as I swallow back my frustration.

"Pretty damn close." My gaze floats to the portrait of my parents hanging over the mantle, and a twinge of guilt settles in my stomach. I can't help but feel like I've failed them. Like I've broken every promise I made.

I thought I was doing the right thing in using my inheritance to finally realize their dreams of hosting weddings on this gorgeous property. Taking out a mortgage on the land in order to construct a quaint inn where wedding guests could stay seemed like a wise investment at the time. We'd already been hosting weddings here, and I was certain I could easily recoup the investment and pay off the mortgage quickly.

Then, almost overnight, the pandemic changed everything. All my plans crumbled when the tourism and wedding industries were hit particularly hard.

Regardless, I still feel like I should be doing more to find a solution, even if I know in my heart I've done everything.

"I won't go down without a fight." My determination returns as I push out all negative thoughts once more.

Thinking about all the what-ifs won't help matters. It's a waste of energy. Instead, I need to focus on what I can do right now to fix things.

"We may not be hosting weddings right now, but more people come to this property during our annual Holley Ridge Christmas Festival than the other eleven months of the year."

"But will that be enough to cover everything?" Estelle presses.

Normally, I wouldn't discuss these kinds of things

with the staff. But Estelle's not really an employee, even if I keep her on the payroll. She's more of a confidant, especially since she was my mother's best friend when she was still alive.

"I'm manifesting only good vibes," I respond, not wanting to admit I'd be lucky if I pulled in a tenth of what I need to come up with when I factor in the increased overhead required to put on the Christmas festival.

Scaling back isn't an option. People come to Holley Ridge this time of year expecting to experience a place full of holiday magic. That's precisely what I plan on giving every single person who walks through these gates.

Even if it's the last year I'll be able to do it.

"The universe will give me what I need."

"Maybe it already has."

I dart my eyes toward Estelle. "What are you talking about?"

"Mr. Tall, Dark, and Handsome in a suit."

"How is *that* the universe giving me what I need?" I refocus my attention on the garland, applying double-sided tape to make sure it doesn't droop along the column.

"When's the last time you've been out on a date, Parker?"

"I don't have time to date."

"Why do you say that?"

I climb down from the ladder, wrapping the last of the garland around the bottom of the column. "Because of this." I gesture around the lobby. "This place takes up all my time."

"Only because you let it. Your staff is more than capable of overseeing things for a few hours, even a few days, without you here. You use this place as an excuse not to have to put yourself out there."

"No, I don't."

"So you haven't been thinking about that handsome man in a suit?"

"I told you, Grandma Estelle. He's just some schmuck trying to buy this place and take advantage of me. The fact he looks absolutely sinful is completely irrelevant. As is the fact that I may have imagined his face when reading my romance novel last night. Or that I may have fantasized about his beard scraping between my thighs, but—"

A loud throat clearing cuts through, and I snap my gaze toward the entryway, my heart dropping to the pit of my stomach when I see none other than Mr. Sex in a Suit, Callum Reed, standing there in the flesh.

"Don't stop on my account. I'd love to hear more," he says, a cocky smirk pulling on his lips.

Fuck. My. Life.

What I wouldn't give to crawl under a rock and not come out until spring.

"A word of advice, dear..." Estelle pats my arm as I remain utterly speechless, embarrassment heating my cheeks. She leans toward me and drops her voice. "If he's trying to fuck you, you may as well enjoy the ride." She passes me a mischievous grin. "If you know what I mean."

FIVE

Callum

"What are you doing here?" Parker asks, obviously flustered.

She pushes a wayward strand of long blonde hair behind her ear. Her cheeks are flushed a light pink as she shifts from foot to foot.

"I thought I made it quite clear I wasn't interested in selling to you." She crosses her arms in front of her chest, holding her head high.

When I walked in and heard her talking about me, I thought it would be a great opportunity to figure out what I'm up against.

I never imagined she was having some of the same thoughts I was.

"That you certainly did, Ms. Holley." I step

toward her, her sweet scent of cinnamon and apples wrapping around me. "But this time I'm not dropping in unannounced. I actually have a reservation."

"You…what?" She can't mask her incredulous tone.

"He called this morning," the older woman interjects with a devilish grin. "Told him all we had left was the wedding cottage. I expected him to balk at the price tag I attached to it."

"And what was that?" Parker narrows her gaze at the woman.

"Two grand a night."

Parker's eyes widen. Then she leans toward her. "That's more than four times what we normally charge, Grandma Estelle. Even during peak nights."

She shrugs dismissively. "I figured if he was willing to pay, may as well let him stay. Screw him out of some money. To my surprise, he was more than happy to pay. For two weeks."

Parker snaps her attention back to me. "Two weeks?"

"I'll leave sooner if you sign those papers."

She pinches her lips into a tight light. "I shredded those papers."

"I brought an extra copy. Several, actually. In case of any future…shredding accidents."

"Well, I'm sorry to disappoint you, Mr. Reed, but

you can stay until this property is ripped from my fingers. I'm still not going to sign those papers."

"Then if I were you, I wouldn't cancel my reservation. Like the lovely Estelle here pointed out, I booked the most expensive accommodation you have. If you want to put a dent into what you owe the bank, this certainly helps. Quite a bit. Plus, I already paid in full. You wouldn't want to have to refund me all that money. Would you?"

"You..." She parts her lips, seemingly searching for the words she needs. The vein in her forehead throbs again, making her look even more beautiful, if that's possible.

"Fine," she eventually relents with an annoyed huff. "You can stay. But only because I want your money. I don't need it, but—"

"Of course you don't." I give her a brilliant smile. "Now, I'd like to check in, Ms. Holley."

"Right this way, Mr. Reed."

She spins on her heels, and I have to stop myself from checking out her ass in those slim-fitting jeans that cling to every delicious inch of her.

"Normally, I'd give you a rundown of our holiday activities," she begins as she takes over for one of her employees at the registration desk, typing at the keyboard. "But seeing as you have zero interest in those—"

"Who says?"

She looks up from the monitor and blows out an annoyed laugh. "Based on our last conversation when you claimed Christmas was a giant waste of resources, *I* do."

I rest my elbow on the wood counter, leaning toward her. "Humor me, Ms. Holley. Maybe you'll help me find my Christmas spirit."

Flirting with her is the absolute last thing I should be doing. I'm here to figure out a way to convince her to sell. Not figure out a way to get into her pants.

I tell myself it's because it's been a while since I've had a woman in my bed. That this has nothing to do with being attracted to her. I *can't* be attracted to her. I'm here to do a job. She's a necessary part of that job. A stepping stone.

Or, more accurately, a blockade.

But a blockade I'll quickly dispense of, no matter the cost.

Which is why I refuse to admit I'm even remotely attracted to her.

But if that were the case, why can't I stop watching her mouth move? Why can't I stop fantasizing about how those lips would taste? Why can't I stop imagining how other parts of her body would taste, too?

"Sounds fun, doesn't it?" Her chipper voice cuts through, yanking me back to the present.

"Loads," I manage to say.

She gives me a disbelieving look. "You didn't hear a word I just said, did you?"

"Of course I did," I lie, not wanting to admit I haven't been able to focus on anything other than her mouth since I walked through the front doors of this inn.

She could have just confessed to killing Kennedy, or knowing what really happened to Amelia Earhart, and I wouldn't have heard a single syllable.

"Christmas and holiday cheer and roasting chestnuts on an open fire."

"Oh, really?" She tilts her head. "So you'd be interested?"

I glance around. Both Estelle and the other front desk employee listen to our conversation with interest, neither of them giving me any indication as to what Parker just said.

The way I see it, this can go one of two ways. I can simply admit I wasn't paying attention because I was fantasizing about how she would taste. That's what a smart person would do. What the voice inside my head tells me to do.

But all my brain cells seem to disappear whenever I'm around this woman.

So instead of doing the smart thing and admitting the truth, I continue playing along.

"Why wouldn't I be? I'm here to have the full Holley Ridge Christmas experience you talked about so animatedly the other day. This is part of that. Isn't it?"

A mischievous glint flashes in her blue eyes, making me sense I'm not going to like whatever I just agreed to.

"Then be in the barn at seven tonight."

I glance down at the piece of paper in front of me that details today's activities, but before I can read any of it, she rips it away.

"Shall I show you to your accommodations now?"

"Certainly."

"Right this way." She skirts out from behind the desk, leading me through the charming lobby.

The wood floors gleam in the afternoon light, the exposed beams above framing a cozy dining area to my right, complete with a view of the mountains rising in the distance. To my left is a bar, the shelves boasting quite a few top-shelf scotches, along with other liquors.

When we emerge onto the veranda, I draw in a deep breath of fresh air, pausing to take in my surroundings. Days ago, this entire area was still under construction, dozens of people helping to string lights and set up booths in the Christmas market. It looks completely different now, the giant Norway spruce decked out for the season, thousands upon thousands of lights strung along various pathways.

I can't fathom the amount of work that goes into

getting this place ready for Christmas every year, the amount of manpower needed not just to hang all these lights but also decorate the tree and construct dozens of huts in the shape of gingerbread houses.

"Mr. Reed?"

I snap my eyes away from the tree, pretending I wasn't just admiring all the effort she went through to transform this property over the past few days.

"You can call me Callum," I tell her as I follow her past the ice skating rink and toward a restored barn near a beautiful lake.

"You're a guest. We treat all our guests with the level of care and service they deserve. That includes addressing them by their last names… Mr. Reed." She grits a smile. "Here. I'll carry that for you." She reaches for the handle of my rolling suitcase.

"I've got it," I insist, keeping it in my grasp.

"Fine." She huffs out an aggravated sigh, and an awkward silence descends on us as we continue along the path.

I can see why people love coming here. Why this place has become a popular location for weddings over the past several years. The rolling hills. The glimmering lake. The mountains in the distance. The lovingly restored barn. It's gorgeous. And based on what little I know of Parker, I have no doubt she does everything she can to make everything perfect for each couple who starts their lives together here. Hell, for everyone who steps foot on this property.

"Here we are." She climbs onto the front porch of a farmhouse-style cottage across a short path from the barn.

"It's charming," I remark as she holds a card up to the keypad. It beeps, granting us entry, and she opens the door, allowing me to step inside.

The interior boasts the same light walls with dark wood accents as in the main building, just on a smaller scale. A fully equipped kitchen with an island sits to the right, a living room complete with stone hearth to the left. Directly ahead of me is a stunning wall of windows with a gorgeous view of the lake that leaves me completely speechless.

"There's a patio out back with a fire pit to keep you warm if you want to sit outside," Parker suggests, noticing where my eyes are currently drawn. "The sunsets are beautiful here, especially in this cottage." The heels of her knee-high boots click on the wood flooring as she moves toward the kitchen. "There are some pots and pans, as well as dishes and silverware. Coffee. Tea. Chocolate. Marshmallows."

"Chocolate and marshmallows?"

"Graham crackers, too. You know. For s'mores. You can't have a fire pit without s'mores."

"If you say so."

She places her hands on her hips, a quizzical look

on her face. "You've never roasted marshmallows for s'mores?"

"I'm not five."

"You don't need to be five to like s'mores. Trust me. There's something quite…delicious about gooey marshmallows and melted chocolate." She licks her lips and closes her eyes, as if imagining enjoying one right now.

But that's not what causes a twitching in my pants.

It's the tiny moan that falls from her throat. It makes me want to slam her against the wall to find out all the ways I can make her moan. I've never been so turned on by a sound before. But hearing Parker's moan unravels me, causing me to clench my fists, jaw tight, nostrils flaring.

And when she opens her eyes and grins mischievously, I sense she knows exactly what she's doing to me.

Of course she does.

"I'll let you get settled." She starts toward the door, pausing as she passes me to add, "Mr. Reed." She lingers for a moment, her delicious scent torturing me with each drawn out second.

Finally, she continues out of the cottage. But before she closes the door, she meets my gaze once more. "Don't forget. Seven o'clock in the barn."

SIX

Parker

"So he's staying?" Haley, my best friend, asks, swirling the deep red wine in her glass as she sits at one of the stools by the bar. "You didn't just turn him away like you did earlier in the week?"

"He booked a reservation. "

I nod at Mr. and Mrs. Zimmerman, the owners of the local pharmacy, as they walk past me. The barn is packed with a mixture of guests and locals seated at the dozen or so high-top tables placed along the perimeter of the dance floor.

"But don't worry. Estelle put him in the cottage. Told him it was the only accommodation we had left."

"You're booked that solid?" Haley's green eyes widen. "That's incredible. That—"

"We're not. That's just what Estelle told him." I glance her way as she mixes an Old Fashioned. "Even gave him a special rate."

"Quadruple the peak rate."

Haley bursts out laughing, the sound carrying through the open space. "That's fantastic."

"What's really fantastic…," Estelle begins, sliding down to our corner of the bar, "is that Mr. Sex in a Suit was so enamored by Parker that she was able to convince him to come tonight."

"Why?" Haley furrows her brow. "I thought you hated him."

"I *do* hate him," I insist. "He's trying to steal this property, for crying out loud."

"He offered you money for it, correct? And quite a lot of it, from what I recall."

"So?"

Truth be told, Callum's offer is extremely generous and will allow me to walk away with a substantial amount in savings, even after paying off all my debts. It will give me freedom to do whatever I want.

But I'm not sure if there's anything else I want to do.

Did I ever see myself owning an inn or hosting weddings? Not really. But after everything my parents did for me, I feel like I owe it to them to make sure their dreams are realized, even if they're not around to see it for themselves. I know they're smiling down on me and are proud of what I've done with Holley Ridge.

"That's not stealing then," Haley remarks.

"Maybe not to you. But to me…" I shake my head, chewing on my bottom lip. "No amount of money is enough. You can't put a price on memories."

"So you duped him into dance lessons in the hopes of…what?" She smooths a strand of auburn hair behind her ear.

"Make him leave. If tonight doesn't work, I'm sure sunrise meditation will do the trick. Or cookie decorating lessons. Or judging the fruitcake competition. This guy hates Christmas. He's about to be immersed in Christmas on steroids. My money's on him cutting bait by the end of the weekend, if he even makes it through the tree lighting ceremony Saturday night."

"What is this? Some twisted holiday version of *How to Lose a Guy in Ten Days*?" Haley takes a sip of her wine.

"And if it is?"

"Then I'm all for it, especially if you get laid."

"Amen, sister." Estelle holds up her hand, and Haley gives her a high five.

"I am *not* sleeping with the enemy." I roll my eyes, although the idea doesn't make my stomach sour like I thought it would.

Truthfully, since Callum Reed checked in, I haven't been able to stop thinking about him. About his woodsy scent. Or the way he seemed on the brink of losing control when I teased him with a little moan. I don't know what came over me. It just sort of…happened. There was just something about the shameless way he raked his gaze over me. And flirted with me. And held his breath whenever I drew near.

"You weren't looking at him like he was the enemy earlier," Estelle points out. "And he certainly wasn't looking at you like you were, either. Don't forget, that's precisely how you were able to swindle him into this."

"Trust me." I brush off her insinuations. "He'll be out of our hair soon. No way is he going to put up with a night of swing dancing just to butter me up to the idea of selling."

"We'll see about that." She waggles her brows as she nods toward the barn entrance.

Haley and I follow her line of sight to see Callum standing there, looking more delicious than he did earlier, if that's even possible. His dark hair is neatly groomed, but in a sexy sort of way, his suit clinging to his body in all the right places. One thing is certain.

Callum Reed knows how to wear a suit. And he wears it so damn well.

"Holy Mr. Sex in a Suit," Haley exhales.

I playfully swat her. "You're not helping."

"Grandma Estelle told me how good looking he was, but damn… He's got to be packing under that."

"I'm guessing a solid six," Estelle states, not taking her eyes off him, as if she has x-ray vision.

"Just six?" Haley arches a brow.

"Darling, six is more than sufficient. All these modern romance novels waxing poetic about a monster pecker don't know what they're talking about."

"Pecker?" I stifle my laugh.

"Have you ever taken out a ruler and seen what eight or ten inches is? That would land me in the hospital. And not because I'm old. There's nowhere for a ten-inch ding-dong to go, other than to impale me in half."

"I could think of worse ways to go than death by penis," Haley responds, as if this were a completely normal conversation. "Especially if the orgasm is commensurate with the size of his ding-dong, as you put it."

"Are we seriously talking about this right now?" I ask through gritted teeth. "I'm trying to run a respectable, family-friendly business, and you two are talking about monster…peckers."

"In the size sense," Estelle clarifies. "Not as in belonging to a literal monster."

Haley tilts her head. "Is that a thing?"

"Oh, sweetie." She places a hand on Haley's forearm. "Monster erotica is most definitely a thing. Alien, too."

"Seriously?"

"I don't joke about my naughty books, sweetie. Do you know what's great about throwing some sort of fantastical creature, like a monster or an alien, into the mix?"

"What's that?" Haley leans closer to Estelle.

"Normal rules don't apply. Anatomically speaking." She gives her a knowing look.

Haley's jaw drops. "You mean…"

"Multiple ding-dongs."

I pinch my eyes shut, feigning annoyance. But if reading monster erotica makes Estelle happy, who am I to yuck on her yum? After over eighty years on this planet, she's earned the right to enjoy whatever she wants.

"When did it become normal to discuss alien or monster sex with Grandma Estelle?" I murmur to no one at all.

"Speaking of monster dicks…" Haley nudges me, nodding toward Callum as he moves in my direction, the crowd seeming to part for him.

"Or, more accurately, one giant dickhead," I

mutter before plastering a congenial expression on my face, ignoring the way my pulse kicks up with every inch he erases between us until he's standing less than a foot away.

"Ms. Holley," he greets cordially.

"Mr. Reed. I'm so glad you could make it. I wasn't sure if you'd actually show up. At the very least, I figured you'd leave once you realized what you'd agreed to when you were ogling me."

"I did no such thing," he argues, not so much of a hint of embarrassment about him.

"The only reason you're here is because you weren't paying attention earlier."

His grin becomes even more playful. Even more devious. Even more sinful.

"I'll admit I was utterly clueless about what you were saying."

"See." I cross my arms in front of my chest, momentarily vindicated.

"But not because I was ogling you."

My arms fall to the side. "You just said—"

"It's because I was watching your mouth move, Ms. Holley." He winks suggestively, and a heat radiates from his stare. "It's a completely different thing. If I ogle you, you'll know." His gaze travels over my body in painstaking slowness, lingering on my chest as he swipes his tongue along his lips.

A fluttering erupts low in my belly, my legs weakening under his intense stare. His eyes scan every inch of my frame, drinking me in like I'm the first source of sustenance he's seen in days or weeks.

"You see, Ms. Holley," he croons, fixating on my lips much in the same manner as he did earlier today. "That was an ogle." His stare burns into me like molten lava, setting every nerve ending in my body ablaze, draining all the air from the room.

Then he steps back, breaking whatever spell he so easily cast over me.

"So, swing dancing?" He glances around the barn.

I clear my throat, taking a moment to compose myself and tell my libido to take a hike before she gets me into trouble.

"As you're aware, Holley Ridge is a popular wedding destination in this area. A few years ago, I got the idea to host dancing lessons for the wedding party and guests as an icebreaker. Over the years, it's grown in popularity, so much so that locals have started to attend. And before you complain that I should charge people for this service, I more than make up for it with the amount the bar takes in during this event. Everyone needs a little liquid courage before putting on their dancing shoes."

He holds up his hands in surrender. "I'm not here to question your business practices."

"I find that hard to believe, considering you had

no problem pointing out what a crappy business-woman I am a few days ago."

"And I shouldn't have done that. You have my deepest apologies."

"I don't know what you think—" I stop short when his words finally register. "What did you say?"

"I said I shouldn't have questioned the way you run things here. I'm sorry."

I open and close my mouth several times, speechless. I didn't think Callum Reed was the type of person who would apologize. He seemed so...harsh and unyielding. A pompous ass who believed he was never wrong.

"Oh. Well. Apology accepted, I suppose."

He gives a subtle nod, but doesn't take his eyes off me. It's unnerving. I can't remember ever being around another man who peered at me with such intensity.

Who made me feel like we were the only two people in the room.

But that's how I feel right now. Even if this man is my sworn enemy.

"May I have your attention, please?"

I snap my eyes away from Callum, watching as Vera, the local high school music teacher, steps up to the front of the room with her husband.

"For those of you from out of town, my name is Vera, and this is my husband, Arnold. We're delighted you're all here. And I promise, by the end of the next hour, you'll all be swing dancing like you've been doing it your entire lives."

The crowd claps politely.

"Now, everyone please pair off. Anyone without a partner, stand on the far wall here, and I'll get you paired up."

"Enjoy your dance class," I say to Callum in a sing-song voice, then turn back toward the bar, wanting to get a good spot to watch him.

Before I can make it more than a few feet, he grabs my forearm, forcing me to stop. My skin heats from the unexpected contact, a delicious tremor rushing through me that increases as I peer into his dark eyes, barely an inch between us.

"Where do you think you're going?" His voice is a low growl that hits me in places I forgot existed.

"I..." I swallow hard, struggling to regain my composure, his proximity overwhelming me. "I'm working the bar."

"I don't think so. You invited me here."

I pull my arm from his hold. "I did nothing of the sort. I simply extended an invitation as part of our daily activities."

"That's not entirely true," Estelle pipes up.

I curse under my breath. For a woman who claims to have trouble hearing, she seems to have no problem when it comes to Callum and me.

I slowly shift my eyes in her direction and shoot daggers.

"You *did* mention you thought it might be a good way for him to get into the holiday spirit. Then you specifically asked if you could count on him to be here. If you ask me, that sounds like more of an individualized invitation."

"Grandma Estelle," I seethe through a tight jaw.

"Precisely the way I took it. If I'm dancing, you are, too." He curves toward me, and I have to fight against the shiver that snakes down my spine. "If you're trying to get rid of me by forcing me into dance lessons, you'll have to try much harder." His voice is deep enough to drown in, sending heat spiraling through me.

Our eyes lock in an unspoken challenge, the atmosphere crackling between us with electricity potent enough to light the entire west coast for years to come. Then he pulls back, that same charismatic smile returning to his face.

"You wouldn't want me to miss out on the full experience of Christmas at Holley Ridge, would you? Considering I'm your highest paying guest, I think I should be entitled to a few additional perks."

"And you consider dancing with me a perk?"

"Absolutely, Ms. Holley." He extends his hand toward me again. "Shall we?"

I lick my lips, searching for anything that can get

me out of dancing with Callum. Touching Callum. Being a whisper away from Callum. This is a disaster waiting to happen.

"The bar!" I exclaim. "I can't leave the bar unattended."

"I'm not dead yet, Parker," Grandma Estelle snips out.

"But dance night can get busy."

"I'll help her," Haley volunteers.

"You don't even work here."

"You're hired," Estelle tells her.

"Goodie!" Haley claps excitedly, making her way behind the counter.

"Problem solved." Estelle beams. "Now go enjoy that…Christmas spirit."

SEVEN

Callum

I don't know what came over me. Why I coerced Parker into being my dance partner for the night.

It was one thing to play along with her scheme to convince me to leave by subjecting me to an activity she assumed I'd never be interested in, especially since most other men are only here because their wives promised something in return for suffering through a night of swing dancing.

Probably a blow job.

It's another thing to spend the night dancing with Parker Holley. This wasn't my intention. I planned to prove to her that she can throw all the cheesy activities she wants at me and it still won't chase me away. Not with millions of dollars on the line.

But the second I laid eyes on her in the knee-length, red dress that clings to her curves before flaring out at the waist, I lost all sense of reason.

"Honestly, if this isn't your thing, you can leave," Parker whispers as we face Vera and Arnold. "No hard feelings or anything."

"I appreciate your concern, but there's something you should know about me."

"What's that?"

"When I commit to something, I don't half-ass it. I go all in. And I'm fully committed to spending the next hour swing dancing with you."

"Then let's see what you've got, Mr. Reed."

"Prepare to be surprised, Ms. Holley."

"Okay everyone." Vera claps, forcing our attention in her direction. "Now that we've got everyone paired up, it's time to start. First, we'll go over the basic step you'll need for your east coast swing. Leads, you'll need to watch Arnold. Follows, keep your eyes on me."

Nearly everyone in attendance watches them with rapt attention. I don't, using the opportunity to take in my surroundings. The restored barn is quite lovely, especially with fairy lights strung overhead, adding to the ambience. I can see why people want to get married here. It has a rustic yet classy charm. And the view is second to none.

It's why I want this property so badly.

"Don't you think you should pay attention?" Parker whispers.

"Don't need to."

"Of course. You're a man, so you're obviously an expert at everything." She rolls her eyes. "Isn't that right?"

"Not everything."

When Vera instructs us to face each other, I turn toward Parker, grabbing her hand in mine and placing my free one just beneath her shoulder, as is customary when doing this specific dance. Music fills the room as Vera counts us down.

"But I *do* know how to dance," I finish, breaking into a rock step, triple step with ease. As if it's second nature.

Once upon a time, it was.

It doesn't matter how many years have passed since I stood in a large room much like this one and did these exact moves. It's like riding a bike. You never truly forget.

Even if I wish I could.

"Who knew the Grinch liked to dance?" Parker says once Vera stops the music.

"It helps me remain limber for stealing all the jing-tinglers and tar-tookas."

"Probably a good idea. Those who-hoopers and blum-bloopers can be pretty heavy," she retorts, catching my reference to a few of the crazy-named toys from the movie I once watched daily during December when I was a child.

"Most definitely." I smile, then look back toward the front of the room as Vera reviews adding a gradual turn to the routine, as well as how to go from open position to closed.

Parker and I practice these additional variations, the two of us moving in perfect sync with the other, as if we've been dancing together much longer than a few minutes.

"Great job everyone." Vera claps to get our attention. "We're going to put it all together now. Just remember, the rock step, triple step is your base. You don't have to do anything else. Just do what you're comfortable with. And most important of all, have fun."

I face Parker, holding my arms out. "Ready to have some fun?"

She steps toward me and takes my hand in hers. "Of course."

The music comes on, and I lead Parker through the basic routine, moving her around the dance floor with ease. After a minute, we progress to a few advanced moves the instructor hasn't reviewed. But Parker still keeps up.

"I have to admit, Mr. Reed. I'm pleasantly surprised."

"With what?" I ask, feigning ignorance.

"You didn't strike me as the type of person to do anything but sit in your office, thinking of ways to steal someone's joy, like the Grinch you are."

A few hours ago, that statement probably would have been filled with venom. I think I'm starting to get under her skin. Helping her see a human side of me instead of simply the person trying to buy this place.

As much as I hate to admit it, maybe Daniel was right. Maybe this is the way to win her over.

"Spend enough time with me and you'll learn I'm full of surprises."

I move us into open position, my arm fully extended as I hold her away from me for a beat. When I pull her back in, I do so with enough force that her body collides with mine, the impact sending a jolt through me that steals my breath.

Not from the motion.

But from the feel of her in my arms, her frame molded so perfectly with mine.

I know nothing about this woman other than the fact that she thinks all she has to do is send positive energy out into the universe and everything will be okay. She's so impractical and carefree, which is everything I'm not.

But my brain doesn't get the message. My gaze hungrily sweeps over her face, lingering on her full lips. As I watch her tongue flick out and swipe over them, it's all I can do to stop myself from leaning forward and capturing her mouth in mine. What I wouldn't give to get a taste of what I've fantasized about since I overheard her talking about what my face would feel like buried between her thighs.

Probably since I first laid eyes on her.

I have a feeling kissing her isn't what Daniel had in mind when he told me to be nice to her. I'm pretty sure that crosses a line and would ruin whatever chance, no matter how small, I have at closing this deal.

Snapping my eyes away from her mouth, I step back into normal position, if for no other reason than so she can't feel how turned on I am right now.

"Where did you learn to dance?" she asks nervously, not looking directly at me as we continue going through the steps, sticking to the basic routine to avoid any further close contact.

"When I was in high school, I moved to a conservative small town where I worked to overturn a ban on dancing so we could have a prom in a barn like this."

She slowly shifts her eyes back to mine, brow furrowed in confusion. Then something incredible happens. Her lips curve into a heartwarming smile as she throws her head back, her laughter echoing in the space. Regardless, her steps don't falter.

I don't think a laugh has ever affected me like this. The way her entire expression brightens stirs something inside of me. The lightness in her eyes. The wrinkle in her nose. The joy consuming her. All because I made her laugh.

I haven't made anyone laugh in years.

"Okay, *Ren*," she replies, easily picking up on the fact that I just gave her the plot to *Footloose*. "And here I assumed it was because some girl forced you to take lessons in preparation for your wedding, only for her to realize what a miserable grump you are and leave you." She laughs slightly, probably expecting me to join her or come back with some snide retort, like I did with the Grinch remarks.

But I have no snide retort.

Instead, her remark freezes me in place, reminding me of the worst time of my life.

"What's wrong?" she asks when I drop my hold on her. "Did you forget it's…" She trails off, realization washing over her. "Oh, shit." She briefly squeezes her eyes shut. "I… Fuck. I'm sorry. I didn't mean anything by it. I just thought of all the reasons someone would take dance classes, then the absolute worst thing that could happen to someone who was engaged or married, but… Oh, Callum." She places her hand on my arm. "I didn't—"

I step back from her touch, squaring my shoulders as I smooth a hand down my suit jacket.

"Thank you for the dance, Ms. Holley," I say, not even able to relish in how amazing it felt to hear her sweet voice call me by my first name. "I enjoyed myself more than I have in a long time."

"Callum, I'm so——"

"Enjoy the rest of your evening," I interrupt, then turn from her, my strides quick and determined as I hurry out of the barn.

EIGHT

Parker

The crisp December air buzzes with holiday cheer as I walk from the inn and toward the lakefront area that's been transformed into the annual Holley Ridge Christmas Festival. Hundreds of people mill about in excited anticipation, their cheeks rosy from the chilly temperatures as they wait for the tree lighting ceremony. By the sheer number of people, it feels like the entire town is here. Further proof that Holley Ridge has become the heartbeat of this small town over the years.

A sense of community surrounds me as people meander down the rows of vendors selling wreaths, ornaments, and other holiday items, the aroma of sugar and nutmeg filling the air from all the sweet treats. Dozens of people stop me as I roam, telling me how beautiful everything is. How they look forward to coming here for this special night all year. How this has become a family tradition, some even driving hours to be here.

It solidifies my resolve not to consider Callum's offer to buy this property. I'll find a way to keep this place afloat, even if it takes a miracle.

If there's any time of year a miracle is possible, it's at Christmas.

"Auntie Parker! Auntie Parker!"

When I hear the tiny voice, I glance to my right as a redheaded little girl runs my way, her curls springing with her steps. Her gray eyes glitter with excitement as she weaves between people's legs, her arms stretched toward me. I crouch down, sweeping her into my embrace as Haley follows close behind.

"Hey, Magpie." I squeeze her tightly, kissing the top of her head.

A frown pulls on the little girl's mouth. "Grandma says no one should call me that. Says my name is Margaret, and that's what people should call me."

I glance at Haley as she fights to hide her annoyance.

I can't say I'm surprised to hear this. Haley's parents are quite...uptight. Her mother nearly had a heart attack when Haley left college to take a job as a flight attendant.

Even more so when she came home to let them know she'd been terminated after getting pregnant by a frequent flier on one of her routes.

Granted, it probably wasn't the smartest idea for her to sleep with him in the first place, but her mother seemed to forget he also played a role in what happened, blaming Haley for seducing a married man.

Even if she had no idea he was married since he never wore a ring.

But Haley was determined to raise her little girl, even after the asshole threw a pile of cash at her so she'd terminate the pregnancy. Her parents did, too. Which is why she tries to limit their involvement in Maggie's life.

"But what do *you* want to be called?" I ask, not giving a shit what her bitch of a grandmother thinks.

Her face lights up. "I like it when you call me Magpie."

I kiss her nose. "Then I proclaim you Lady Magpie of Holley Ridge."

She squeals excitedly, and I set her on her feet.

"It looks beautiful, Parker," Haley says, giving me a hug.

I swallow hard as I shift my gaze over the grounds, a pang squeezing my heart that this may be the last tree lighting ceremony I ever hold here. But I quickly push those thoughts away.

"Thanks, sweetie."

"They'd be proud of you. No matter what happens."

I give my best friend another hug, then meander through the festival with her, soaking it all in.

"How's the apartment hunt going?" I keep my voice low so Maggie can't overhear. I doubt she would anyway, considering she's currently pre-occupied with all the lights and decorations.

"Not great." Haley heaves a sigh. "The downside of living in a small town. There's not many rentals to begin with, and what *is* available is over my budget. This may come as a surprise, but I'm not exactly raking it in as a dog walker and cocktail waitress."

"From what I understand, Beckham Lawrence still rents out his townhouse. You could always see if it's available."

"Beckham Lawrence? Are you crazy? Absolutely not. There's no way he'd do me any favors, like rent to me, especially when I wouldn't be able to pay him anywhere close to what he can get for a short-term rental."

I've always wondered what the story is between the head winemaker at one of the vineyards here in Sycamore Falls and my best friend. She's always insisted there isn't one. That they knew each other as kids, since her nanny was good friends with his mom, but they went their separate ways as they got older.

But I see the way he looks at her.

And how he looks at her little girl.

That's not someone who hates Haley.

Unfortunately, she's too stubborn to admit it.

"You'll never know if you don't ask. I'd offer you my spare bedroom, but it may not be mine much longer."

"It will be." She squeezes my hand. "I can feel it."

"Thanks, Haley." I give her one more hug, then politely excuse myself, continuing toward the makeshift stage at the foot of the enormous tree as the local high school choir entertains the crowd with a rendition of "I'll Be Home for Christmas".

Once the song comes to an end, I climb up the steps and make my way toward the microphone. Warmth fills me as I take in all the people here for tonight's ceremony.

"Hello friends and Merry Christmas."

Everyone claps and cheers, smiles lining their faces, many familiar, some not.

"I'm not going to stand up here and bore you with a long speech. I don't actually have one prepared. Every year, I tell myself I'll jot down what I want to say. And every year, I end up winging it. Just like my parents did. My dad once told me there was something magical about letting the moment dictate what to do or say. And this is one of my favorite moments of the year, being able to look out over this crowd and see all these familiar faces that have made it a tradition to come to Holley Ridge the first Saturday of December to celebrate the start of the Christmas season."

A feeling of nostalgia fills me as I recall standing out in that crowd and watching my parents up here. At the time, I was just a foster kid whose only wish was to have a home for Christmas. I never could have imagined that next year, this place would become my home.

"One of my earliest childhood memories is standing out where you are, waiting to finally see the tree all lit up," I continue. "Walking through the festival and smelling all the delicious smells. Waiting in line to see Santa. Singing Christmas carols with the choir. It was all so magical.

"And the second my dad flicked the switch, and the tree lit up..." I shake my head, my chest expanding from the memory. "It's hard to explain how that made me feel, especially as a small child. It's a memory I will always keep with me, no matter what the future holds. Just like I hope you all hold dear the memories you make tonight."

Another round of polite clapping fills the air, several people in the crowd hugging or kissing.

Once the applause dies down, I clear my throat. "Now, without further ado, I give you the Holley Ridge Christmas Tree."

I walk toward the switch by the tree and flip it, the tree lighting up the night sky, the choir belting out "O Christmas Tree".

While everyone's attention is drawn to the towering Norway spruce dozens of community volunteers carefully helped decorate over the past several days, mine remains focused on the crowd, wanting to remember everything about the way they admire the tree.

Families snuggle together. Couples share an embrace. There are even a few heartfelt kisses as people allow the spirit of the season to fill them with joy.

But as I continue scanning all the faces, I notice one person standing alone off to the side, as if he doesn't belong.

As much as I initially hoped to chase Callum off with an overabundance of holiday cheer, I can't help but feel bad for him. Not just because I don't believe anyone should be alone at Christmas, but because of the way he shut down when I joked about him having to take dance classes for a wedding that didn't end well. Or maybe never even happened. I didn't mean anything by it.

Based on his reaction, I sense there was a certain level of truth to my words. I should have brushed it off. Forgotten about it and focused on finding a way to save Holley Ridge. Instead, all I've thought about since then has been Callum Reed and the reason behind his sudden departure the other night.

A part of me wants to believe he deserves being dumped and left heartbroken. But the compassionate side of me — which is technically all of me, apart from the tiny sliver reserved for people trying to screw me over — feels for him. I know what it's like to feel all alone. To think you don't have anyone.

I climb down the stage and skirt through the crowd, accepting congratulations from everyone I pass. I don't linger, though, wanting to get to Callum before he decides all this holiday cheer is too much and leaves.

The thought surprises me, considering less than forty-eight hours ago, I wanted him to leave and never show his face here again.

"So what's the verdict?" I ask as I approach, his eyes focused on the tree, as if memorizing every twinkling light and ornament.

"It's quite…"

"Excessive? Superfluous? Pointless?"

He shifts his gaze from the tree, the reflection of all the lights sparkling within his dark orbs. Then a soft smile tugs on his mouth.

"Beautiful, Parker. It's absolutely beautiful."

I bite on my lower lip, fighting against the grin wanting to break free. I've never cared about anyone's approval or praise. For some reason, I want that from

Callum. Want to think I've finally opened his eyes and made him understand why this place is so important.

It's not just the land or the property. Or even the business. It's this feeling. Giving people a moment of joy in their hectic lives. And hopefully, they can bring that feeling home with them. Let it last until the next holiday season.

Quickly tearing my eyes from his, I step back, clearing my throat. "I wanted to apologize for the other night."

"There's nothing to apologize for," he insists, but the tight set of his jaw indicates it still bothers him, even if he's trying to pretend otherwise.

"I think there is. So…I'm sorry." I hold out my hand. "Truce?"

With a furrowed brow, he eyes my hand for a protracted beat. Finally, he places his gloved one in mine and we shake. "Truce."

I ignore the shiver that runs through me as I meet his gaze again, blaming it on the chill in the air, despite the fact we're standing by a heater.

Pulling my hand back, I look away, wrapping my arms around myself. "It's probably a good thing you left early, anyway."

"Why's that?"

"After a few hours of dancing, we typically break out the karaoke machine. You'd probably hate every-thing about that."

"Have you already forgotten what I told you the other night?"

"What's that?"

He steps closer, his proximity causing my heart rate to kick up, those damn butterflies making themselves known.

"I'm just full of surprises." He lingers near me for a moment, my gaze transfixed by his lips. I wonder what they'd taste like. If he kisses with all the tenacity and determination he seems to devote to every other aspect of his life.

He admitted he doesn't half-ass anything. I have no doubt his kiss would be persistent, demanding, and so damn thorough it would ruin me for any man to come after him.

"I actually quite like karaoke." Callum pulls back, his voice snapping me out of my growing inappropriate thoughts. "At least the part of watching people make utter fools of themselves, which is bound to happen when alcohol is involved, at least in my experience."

"It is great entertainment." I smooth a wayward blonde curl behind my ear, pretending I hadn't been fantasizing about how Callum would kiss. A part of me thinks maybe I should just press my mouth to his and find out. Get him out of my system.

Something tells me he's not the kind of man you can kiss or even fuck out of your system.

"It's why I do it," I add when he remains unnervingly quiet. "Granted, I'm surprised by the pipes on some people. Others… Well, everyone thinks they'll be the next Taylor Swift after a few drinks."

"I'm sorry I missed it. Maybe next week."

I nod subtly. "Next week."

"Unless you manage to chase me away before then."

"Right. Of course."

Several moments of awkward silence pass as we keep our eyes trained on the tree, neither one of us seeming to know how to act around each other. I try to remind myself he's just a guest. I normally have no problem striking up a random conversation with anyone who visits Holley Ridge, regardless of whether they've lived in Sycamore Falls their entire life or it's their first time visiting.

But Callum Reed unnerves me.

"Well, I should get—" I begin.

"Would you like to—" he says at the same time, both of us laughing nervously. Then he lifts his gaze to mine. "You first."

"I was just going to say I should get back to work. Check on everything to make sure it's all running smoothly." I gesture at the crowds, a line forming for horse-drawn carriages and the ice-skating rink, not to mention for photos with Santa.

Truthfully, I could probably get away with

spending some time with Callum. I have my radio and cell phone in case anything comes up.

I just don't think it's a good idea for me to be around him more than necessary. Not when he looks at me like he has been tonight.

Like he did the other night, too.

"Of course. Thank you for taking the time to talk to me. As always, your company has been quite enjoyable."

"What were you going to say?"

"Nothing," he answers quickly, increasing the space between us. "Enjoy your evening, Ms. Holley."

With one last glance my way, he turns from me, making his way from the festivities and along the path toward his cottage.

All alone.

NINE

Parker

"How's our guest of honor doing?" Grandma Estelle asks as I curl the ribbon on the end of a bouquet of balloons, setting the weight anchoring them in the center of one of the dozen tables.

Over the past several hours, my staff has helped to transform the barn into a wonderland for kids, complete with both a cotton candy and popcorn machine. The tables overflow with treats — colorful candies, chocolates wrapped in festive foil, cupcakes with swirls of buttercream frosting, and skillfully decorated gingerbread men.

"As far as I know, he's doing well."

"And he's still here?" she presses, despite knowing the answer.

Even if she hasn't seen him walking around the property like I have, she could easily log into the reservation system and see he still shows as a registered guest.

"He is."

"Hmm."

"What?" I snap my eyes toward her as she moves down a line of goodie bags, adding a container of putty into each one.

"The way you were talking the other night, I figured he'd be gone by now. You seemed quite insistent you were going to chase him away with all the Christmas frivolity."

I shrug, following Estelle with fidget toys and placing one in each bag. "He's harmless."

Estelle comes to an abrupt stop, causing me to almost ram into her. "You like him, Parker Ellen Holley."

I roll my eyes, avoiding her stare. "That's ridiculous. He's the enemy, remember?"

Although he doesn't feel like the enemy anymore. He hasn't since we danced together.

Granted, I haven't spoken to him much over the past few days, apart from the tree lighting ceremony. But I've seen him roaming the ridge and watched with a little too much interest as he took photos of the various Christmas decorations. Or as he listened to a local a cappella group sing Christmas carols. Or as he joined some of my father's friends in their daily chess game on the veranda.

The animosity overwhelming me when he first showed up here has decreased. All because I caught a glimpse of the human side he'd been hiding beneath his gruff, uncaring exterior.

But should that make any difference? He still wants to buy this place from me. Then again, it's not like he's trying to screw me over. If anything, he's trying to help me out of this impossible position I'm in. I know selling is the smart thing to do. I'm just not sure if I can give up on my parents' ranch. Not yet. Not until there's no chance of saving it.

"He didn't look like the enemy when you two were dancing together the other night," Estelle remarks, pulling me out of my conflicted thoughts. "The chemistry was straight fire."

"Straight...fire?" I repeat, wondering where Grandma Estelle heard that term.

"Haley thought so, too."

"Don't pull Haley into this. She's not here to corroborate."

"Do you want me to call her? She'll tell you the same thing. There's something there between you two."

"He's a guest here. Soon, he'll be gone and I'll never have to see him again. If you ask me, that day can't come soon enough. So if you don't mind—"

My statement is interrupted when the door bursts open. Claire, one of my front desk employees, barrels toward me. Her face is flushed with panic as she struggles to catch her breath, probably having run all the way out here from the inn.

"Oh, god. What happened?" I ask, unsure if I can handle whatever she's about to tell me. I don't need any more bad news or surprises right now.

"Nothing happened. Well, nothing disastrous."

"Okay...," I draw out. "Then what's going on?"

"Mrs. Cromwell just called. Said that George has been down with a stomach bug for the past twenty-four hours. Pretty nasty one, too. I'm so sorry, Parker. He won't be able to make it today."

I squeeze my eyes shut, a knot forming in my throat. "But he's supposed to be Santa. We can't have a meet and greet with Santa without the jolly man dressed in red."

"Mrs. Cromwell felt horrible. So did George. They know how important this is to you. But he doesn't want to get any of the kids sick. Plus, he can't even keep water down right now."

"It's okay. I just..." I pinch my lips together, mentally going through my staff to see if there's anyone I can convince to play Santa for an hour. I'm short-handed as it is, having decided not to hire any temporary holiday help this year, considering my circumstances.

Plus, I don't have money in the budget to pay someone. George has played Santa at Holley Ridge for years, refusing to accept any payment, since he was such a good friend of my dad's.

"I can see if Finn or one of the other guys at the fire department is available," Claire suggests. "He's best friends with my sister. He'd do it if he's around."

I consider her proposal for a beat. At this point, I'll take any warm body. But before I can say as much, Estelle pipes in.

"I know someone you can ask."

"Who?" I whip my eyes toward her. And when I see the smirk crawling on her lips, I know precisely who she's thinking about.

"A certain guest staying here."

"I can't ask him to do that."

"I thought you planned to inundate him with so much Christmas cheer, he'd flee this place faster than a reindeer on a pair of rollerblades. Playing Santa would most certainly do that." She crosses her arms, a mischievous glint lighting up her gray eyes. "Unless you've changed your mind and want him to stay."

"This is too important to let someone like Callum Reed help."

"Do you have any other options?"

"I..." I stare into space, trying to think of someone — *anyone* — who will fit into the Santa suit that was specially made to fit George Cromwell's larger-than-life physique, thanks to his years spent in the Marines.

Other than a couple of the guys in the fire department, only one man comes to mind.

Hanging my head, I push out a long sigh. "I'll go talk to him." Then I turn my attention to Claire. "In the meantime, call Finn. See if he can spare an hour."

"Sure thing, Parker."

Then I make my way out of the barn on a mission to ask the biggest grump I know to play Santa.

TEN

Callum

I stare at the pieces on the chess board as I sit underneath a heater on the veranda, trying to predict all possible outcomes of whatever move I make next.

Since I came to Holley Ridge with the intention of winning Parker over with my charm, this has become my favorite part of the day. I never thought I'd be the type of person to slow down and spend hours playing chess with a bunch of older locals.

But after they invited me to join them on my second day here, this has become part of my routine. Much like it's a part of theirs.

I also like how it allows me to catch a glimpse of Parker on occasion, more so than if I stayed in my cottage, reviewing proposals and reports on my firm's current projects. Which is precisely what I should be doing.

I tell myself the reason I'm not is to make sure I close this deal. I can't do that by remaining cooped up in the cottage.

The truth is, I don't want to miss a single opportunity to see Parker, even if for only a second.

Deciding that none of my potential moves outweigh another, I take a chance and advance my knight, then lean back into my chair, watching as Bernie, my partner for the day, analyzes the board for several moments.

As he pushes one of his pawns forward, a flash of blonde hair catches my attention.

Hell, I'm pretty sure it catches everyone else's attention, too. It's kind of hard not to stare at Parker as she hurries toward us, her body clad in a green elf costume, a pair of candy-cane leggings accentuating her long legs. The jingle of bells on her hat accompanies the clicking of her black heels.

It's official. I now have a new appreciation for the Christmas season.

"Mr. Reed," she says, slightly out of breath as she approaches me. I have to fight the urge to throw my coat over her so none of the other guests can ogle her, especially when I notice a couple in their twenties pass, the man's eyes lingering on Parker longer than I like.

I shouldn't be jealous over the idea that other people are looking at her. I can't help but feel somewhat possessive of her. I don't want anyone checking her out. I want to be the only one who gets to see her looking as incredible as she does.

Her costume isn't even that sexy or revealing.

That doesn't stop my brain from imagining all the fun we could have in private.

My naughty little elf.

"Is everything okay?" I push back from the table and stand, discreetly adjusting myself.

"I…" She chews on her lower lip.

Which doesn't help matters.

It makes me want to chew on her lip, too. Find out if it's as delicious as I've imagined.

"Can I talk to you for a moment?"

"Sure." I look at Bernie. "I'll be right back."

"Take your time, son," he says with a mischievous grin.

I shake my head, knowing the guys will definitely tease me about this later. They already pester me about her as it is, considering they've picked up on the fact that the second she's in view, I become distracted and make horrible decisions, which have sometimes cost me the game.

"Is everything okay?" I ask again once we're on the opposite side of the veranda.

"I—" She stops short as she scans my frame, a furrow creasing her brow. "Are *you* okay?"

"Why do you ask?"

"I figured you were born wearing a dark suit. I didn't think you owned something as provincial as jeans and a sweater."

"I didn't get my first suit until I was at least a few hours old." I wink.

"Of course."

Admittedly, I much prefer wearing suits. They're like a coat of armor. They make me feel like I can accomplish whatever I need. But my new friends mentioned Parker preferred a more rugged kind of man. Not someone who wore suits all the time.

So I started to dress more casually.

I'd like to say it was to earn her trust. Help her see me as someone she might want to do business with.

Another part of me wanted this precise reaction. For her to rake her gaze over me as she held her breath, her pupils flaming.

"What can I do for you?" I ask after a protracted beat.

"Oh, right. Sorry." She snaps her eyes back to mine and draws in a deep inhale. "I'll preface this by saying if there was anyone else I could ask, I wouldn't be doing this. Unfortunately, there isn't and I'm just desperate enough to ask for your help, even if I'll most likely regret this later."

"What is it?"

"I was wondering if you'd be Santa." Her face squeezes in timid apprehension.

"Santa?" I repeat, making sure I heard her correctly. "Is this another ploy for you to convince me to leave? Because if you couldn't scare me away with dancing, I doubt—"

"Not at all. I swear to you. If it were for a normal photo opportunity, I wouldn't even bother. But this afternoon is the kid's carnival."

"Kid's carnival?"

"Every year, I invite over a hundred area foster kids to the ranch for some holiday cheer. This time of year can be difficult for them. The kids get to meet Santa, something many of them aren't able to do without this opportunity."

I blink repeatedly. "They don't get to meet Santa otherwise?"

"You know what? Forget it." She huffs out a breath, the vein in her forehead throbbing in irritation. "I should have known you wouldn't give a shit. Grinch."

She spins, her blonde waves practically whipping me from the force of her abrupt movement. But before she can retreat, I grab her arm, pushing down the jolt of electricity that shoots through me from the contact, regardless of the barrier of our clothing.

"I didn't mean it like that. I just… It didn't dawn on me that some kids don't get to meet Santa."

She yanks her arm free from my hold. "Well, when you don't have money, or are in foster care, you miss out on a lot of stuff most kids take for granted. Like meeting Santa. So if you'll excuse me, I need to find someone to be Santa so these kids can experience one good thing this holiday season."

She storms off, my new friends watching us with interest. As if this is the most exciting thing to happen in months.

It probably is.

It's much more exciting than listening to Walter tell us about the ingrown toenail he had removed last week.

"I'll do it," I call out before I can stop myself.

Parker skids to a halt, not moving for several moments. Then she slowly faces me.

"Are you sure?" She steps toward me, her voice low. "This is really important to me, Callum. I don't need you to agree to this, then tell these kids Santa isn't real and that all this Christmas stuff is bullshit. Trust me. That is the last thing they need when their hope in anything good is hanging by a thread as it is."

I approach her, not willing to admit I'd agree to

anything if it meant I could hear her call me Callum again.

"I would never do that." I push a wayward curl behind her ear. "Every kid deserves to believe in Santa."

Our eyes lock. "Yes, they do."

"Just promise me one thing."

"What's that?"

I lean toward her. "That you change out of your outfit."

She furrows her brow, glancing down her body. "But this is my elf costume. I wear it every year for the kid's carnival."

"And I appreciate that. But if you're going to be in the same room where I'm playing Santa and having kids sit on my lap, I *really* need you to wear something else."

"Why?" The crease on her forehead grows even more pronounced. "I don't…" She trails off, her eyes widening, jaw going slack as the realization hits her. "Oh." She bites on her lower lip again, trying to fight against her smile. A blush blooms on her cheeks, and I have a feeling it has nothing to do with the chilly temperature.

She lifts her eyes back to mine. "Okay, Mr. Reed. I'll change into something else."

"Thank you." I expel a relieved breath, grateful I won't permanently scar any kids today.

Then again, Parker Holley could probably wear a paper sack and I'd be just as attracted to her.

ELEVEN

Parker

"Enjoying the view?" Estelle sidles up to me as I take a break mid-party to appreciate how happy all the kids seem.

I snap my attention away from Callum, having been admiring him for the past few seconds. And not simply to make sure he doesn't act out. But because of the way he easily interacts with all the kids, as if it's second nature.

I expected him to merely go through the motions of being Santa, like I instructed him. Pose for photos, but don't speak too much.

It took him a few minutes, but he eventually got into the role, asking the kids if they were good. Even those who claimed they weren't sure, a common theme among foster kids, he assured them they're being too hard on themselves.

There was a time I would have given anything for someone like Callum to tell me that. To give me the hope he instilled in many of the kids today.

"Just making sure he doesn't ruin this for anyone."

Estelle places a hand on my arm. "You know he won't. He's a good person."

"Who's trying to steal Holley Ridge."

"Doesn't look like he's trying to steal the ridge right now," she snips back with a hint of superiority. "If anything, it looks like he's *helping* you."

"It's probably all part of his scheme to make me think he's a decent human being."

"If you ask me, he is." She glances at Callum as he talks animatedly with a little boy about his favorite video games. "He didn't have to agree to this. Yet he's doing it anyway. I think that should count for something." She pins me with a stare, then turns, walking toward the arts and crafts station to help kids make Christmas ornaments.

"Maybe so," I murmur, shifting my eyes toward Callum once more.

As I do, he glances away from the little boy, his gaze briefly locking with mine. It could just be the costume, but I swear I see a twinkle in his dark eyes.

The next few hours pass in a whirlwind of food

and games, which is a blessing in disguise. It helps distract me from thinking about Callum Reed. And the heat in his stare as he told me he needed me to change out of my elf costume if he was to play Santa.

Which I did.

But I may have intentionally chosen another slim-fitting dress just to see his reaction.

Once the last kid has left, I approach Callum, surprised to see him helping clean everything up.

"You don't have to do that," I tell him. "You've already done more than enough."

And he did. I told him he could leave after all the kids had their pictures taken. He didn't, though, staying to play games, like pin the nose on Rudolph and the marshmallow relay race. He even helped the smaller kids with the piñata.

"I don't mind." He passes me a smile I shouldn't find as sexy as I do.

But it's impossible not to with the Santa jacket hanging open, revealing a fitted white t-shirt that clings to his muscles. He's ditched the hat and beard, his facial hair dusted with powder to help it blend in with the fake beard he wore.

Which makes him look a bit like a silver fox.

And silver-fox Callum is too sexy for his own good.

"Thanks for today." I help him return all the craft

supplies to their appropriate bins. "It meant a lot to me. And the kids."

He meets my gaze. "Like I said earlier. All kids deserve to believe in the magic of Santa."

"Yes, they do." My lips lift in the corners.

I barely recognize the brooding man who stood in my office last week, telling me Christmas was a waste of time and resources. I just wish I could tell if it's because he's had a change of heart or if it's all an act to get me to sell to him.

"Well, thanks again." I grab a few of the containers and start toward the doors.

"The letters," Callum calls after me. "What are they for?"

I pause, turning to face him. "What do you mean?"

He closes the distance between us. "You made sure every kid wrote a letter to Santa. And I noticed you cross referencing them when the kids were playing games. Why?"

I shrug. "All those kids… Santa doesn't visit their houses. Not unless I do something to help. So that's what those lists are for."

"You buy them presents?"

"I know what you're going to say," I scoff, rolling my eyes. "That it's a waste of resources, considering this place is so far in the red right now it's laughable. But I'd sooner stop paying every single one of my bills before I stop making sure each of those kids gets at least one present from Santa.

"You look at this place and see excess and commercialization. But that's not what Christmas is about. Not to me. It's not about the tree or the lights or the decorations. It's about bringing joy to those who've had their lives turned upside down. Who are on the brink of losing all hope. Who think no one cares about them. This is why I can't give up without a fight. Because I can't give up on them." My voice quivers slightly, and I curse myself for showing emotion around him.

For allowing him a peek beneath the surface.

"Now if you'll excuse me." I grit a smile, then spin, my steps determined as I hurry away from him.

"Would you like to have dinner with me?" he calls out just as I'm about to slip through the open barn doors.

I come to an abrupt stop, his question slamming into me like a boulder. I glance over my shoulder.

"I beg your pardon?"

He slowly advances toward me, each inch he erases causing my heart to beat a little faster, the warmth in his eyes holding me captive.

"I'd like to take you to dinner," he says evenly. Calmly. Confidently.

"D-dinner?"

"To discuss a few things pertaining to the property," he adds quickly. "I know you have your reservations about selling to me. But I'd like to see if we can meet somewhere in the middle."

"I don't—"

"I understand you're…manifesting a solution to magically fall into your lap. But in case it doesn't, maybe it's in both of our best interests to see if we can come to a compromise. It's obvious you care about this property and don't want to entertain the idea of losing it. But isn't it better if it went to the devil you know versus the one you don't who snags it at auction for pennies on the dollar?"

I part my lips, torn about whether to agree. He *does* have a point.

I can manifest for the universe to provide me with a solution but still be smart enough to explore other options. And Callum seems willing to listen to my concerns regarding his initial proposal, which is more than I can say for him last week.

But another part of me knows nothing good can come from this. Not when I already find myself thinking about him more than I should.

This was easier when there was a wall between us. When I vilified him as the grump trying to steal Christmas at Holley Ridge.

It's different now that he's proven himself capable of being a decent human.

"It's just dinner," he continues, moving toward

me. "Nothing more. If it makes you feel better, you can call it a business meeting with food."

Every voice in my head tells me this isn't a good idea. But something about his pleading expression coupled with how sexy he looks with that Santa jacket hanging off him has me ignoring all rationale.

After all, he did me this favor. The least I can do is go to dinner and listen to his proposal.

"Okay."

As soon as the word leaves my mouth, a brilliant smile spreads across his face, like the first ray of sun peeking through the clouds after a storm. For being so cantankerous, Callum Reed has a gorgeous smile.

He should do it more often.

"Can you be ready by seven?"

"Tonight?" My eyes grow wide.

"I figured it's easier for you to take a few hours off in the middle of the week, since you start getting busier on Thursday. Correct?" He arches a brow, and I nod. "Then tonight it is."

He rakes his eyes down my frame. Not in a creepy way. In a way that makes me feel more appreciated than I have in a while.

"I'll meet you in the lobby?"

"See you there," I respond quickly.

"Can't wait." He treats me to that breathtaking smile once more. "Oh, and Parker?"

"Yes?"

"Wear a dress."

"Is there a reason for that?"

"Your legs are a work of art and shouldn't be hidden underneath pants." He holds my gaze for a beat, then continues out of the barn.

What the hell did I just agree to?

TWELVE

Parker

"So, it's a date then," Haley remarks after I finish telling her about Callum's proposition as she lounges on the couch in my living room, a glass of wine in her hand.

"It's a business dinner." I straighten my spine, but don't look directly at my friend. "He said he wants to listen to my reservations about his proposal and see if we can reach a compromise in the event I'm unable to come up with the funds I need."

"Is that what they're calling it these days?" She waggles her brows.

"I need to do something, Haley." I swallow hard through the ball of desperation forming in my throat. "Sure, we were booked solid for the tree lighting ceremony. And I'm almost full the next few weekends. But it won't be enough. I should at least listen to what he has to say in the event the universe is all out of miracles right now."

I slip inside my bedroom and grab the two dresses I'm debating between, holding them up to me as I return to the living room. "Now, which one should I wear?"

"You sure this isn't a date? Because neither of those scream business meeting."

I frown, looking down at the dresses. "They don't?"

"They scream 'you'll be ripping this off me in a few hours.'"

The dresses aren't that sexy. One's a fitted black dress that falls right above my knee with a slit running up one side. The other is a plum wrap dress that hits at my mid-thigh. It's shorter than my little black dress, but is probably a bit more fun.

"I'll go with the plum," I announce, turning from her and disappearing into my bedroom, shedding my robe.

"Did you shave?" she calls out.

"It's a business meeting," I reply as I slip my arms through the sleeves of the dress. "But yes. I shaved."

"Everywhere?"

"That's none of your business."

There's no way I'm going to tell her the truth.

That I did spend some time catching up on my personal grooming.

"It's totally a date."

"You don't hear me pestering you about a certain head winemaker I noticed you talking to during the tree lighting ceremony." I tie the fabric belt of my dress into a bow, then check my reflection in the full-length mirror.

The shade of the dress makes my blue eyes appear slightly more purple than usual, especially with the smoky eyeshadow framing them. I'm not one to wear much makeup, preferring more of a natural look to go with my signature red lips. It just seems like the thing to do tonight.

"How many times do I have to tell you? We hate each other. But Maggie loves Beckham. At least, she loves all the pretty pictures on his arms, as she calls them."

"And how do *you* feel about all the pretty pictures on his arms?"

"Honestly, I couldn't care less about his tattoos."

I can hear the lack of conviction in her voice. I'd bet she's probably thinking about them right now. And not in a PG-rated sense, either.

"Did you talk to him about renting his townhouse?"

"Not yet. I didn't think the tree lighting ceremony

was the right time, considering I had Maggie with me."

"But you *are* going to, right?"

"I think I owe it to Maggie to…" she trails off, her eyes widening when I step back into the living room. "Woah."

"*Good* woah, or *what were you thinking* woah?"

"This is totally a date, Parker. You look straight fire."

"So that's where Grandma Estelle got it from."

"Are you wearing matching underwear and bra?" She stands from the couch and heads toward me. "And is it sexy?"

"That's completely irrelevant." I swipe my wine glass off the kitchen island and throw back a healthy gulp, needing it to help settle my mounting nerves.

"You totally are. Aren't you?"

I roll my eyes, not about to admit that I *am* wearing matching bra and panties. And they are quite sexy.

I don't often have an opportunity to dress up like this. Even though this is decidedly not a date, I can still do something to feel sexy.

For myself.

Not for Callum Reed.

Definitely not for Callum Reed.

"As much fun as this has been, I need to get

going." I glance at the clock on the stove. "I'm already late."

"Fine. But I expect a full report tomorrow. Especially if Estelle was right."

I furrow my brows. "About what?"

"That he's packing a monster cock." She giggles.

"Not a date," I remind her as I grab my coat and purse, taking a moment to collect myself. Then I make my way out of my on-site apartment and down the administrative corridor, Haley following me.

When I reach the lobby, a part of me hopes Callum isn't here. Or that he left word with Claire at the front desk that something came up and he can't make it.

Instead, I feel him the second I walk into the cozy space, subtle jazz renditions of Christmas classics adding to the romantic ambience. He's standing by the tree, looking at all the twinkling lights, a fire roaring in the fireplace.

As if able to sense my presence, he immediately turns my way. His lips part, eyes flaming as he takes in my appearance, the air between us growing thick.

He may have ogled me last week, but this is so much more than that. I've never had another man look at me the way Callum admires me. As if he's never seen anyone so beautiful.

And truth be told, I've never seen anyone as beautiful, either. Especially since he traded his typical dark suit for a navy blue one. Instead of a boring, plain tie like he typically wears, he's donned a red one with a few snowflakes. It's subtle and not over the top. But the fact it's festive is a huge step.

"Yup," Haley whispers in my ear. "It's totally a date."

I glance at her, about to protest once more, but before I can, she cuts me off.

"Have fun." She gives me a quick squeeze, then hurries toward where Maggie is doing a puzzle with Grandma Estelle, leaving me alone with Callum.

Well, technically, there are a few other guests around, as well as Claire at the registration desk. But when Callum slowly moves toward me, his eyes not leaving mine for even a heartbeat as they drink me in, it feels like we're the only two people in the room.

"You look beautiful." He leans toward me, and I hold my breath as he brushes a soft kiss to my cheek. It's an innocent gesture, similar to one shared by family.

But there is absolutely nothing innocent about my reaction to the feel of Callum's lips on my skin. Every nerve in my body comes alive as heat radiates through me, reawakening parts of me I forgot existed.

When he pulls back, I do my best to appear unaffected. But it's impossible with the electricity coursing through my veins, lighting me on fire.

"I... I like your tie."

I like your tie? That's all I could come up with? Nice one, Parker.

"I've been doing some shopping in town. Supporting the local businesses and whatnot. I figured you'd appreciate it."

"I certainly do."

But not as much as I appreciate what's going on underneath that tie.

"Are you ready?" he asks after a beat.

"Of course."

I start to put my coat on, but he steps toward me, taking it from me.

"Allow me."

For being such a grump, he's quite the gentleman.

Then again, I'm beginning to realize he's not as grumpy as I originally thought.

"My car's out front." He extends his arm toward the main entrance.

"We can walk. Main Street is just around the corner. Parking downtown can be difficult this time of year."

"We're not staying in town."

"We're not?"

He slowly shakes his head. "No."

"Where are we going?"

"You'll find out."

I'm on the brink of insisting I can't leave

Sycamore Falls for hours on end in case there's an emergency.

But Estelle is right. I deserve a night off once in a while. My staff is well-trained and can handle anything that may come up. So instead, I allow Callum to lead me out to his car for our business meeting.

Which is most definitely not a date.

THIRTEEN

Callum

Parker's eyes sparkle with excitement as we stroll along the sidewalk in a charming Dutch-inspired town an hour later, taking in every sight, sound, and smell. All the buildings are outlined in glittering white lights, more hanging from nearby trees and lampposts. There's a chill in the air, as if it's about to snow.

At first, I wasn't sure where to bring her tonight. I could have met her for dinner at her inn. Or at one of the restaurants in Sycamore Falls.

But based on what I've picked up from her staff over the past week, she works all the time. Granted, I do, too, but Holley Ridge has become her life to the point that she rarely leaves the property unless it's to run an errand. She even lives in an apartment on the premises.

If anyone deserves a break, she does.

Plus, I wanted to take her somewhere we could discuss my offer without her being surround by memories. Somewhere more…neutral.

"This is us," I tell Parker, opening the door to a quaint restaurant attached to a hotel, delicious aromas invading my senses the second we step inside.

"You didn't have to go through all this trouble," she says for what feels like the hundredth time in the past hour. "I would have been fine staying in town."

"What fun is that?" I reply, then give the hostess my name.

"Right this way, Mr. Reed," she says with a smile, leading us past dozens of couples exchanging flirtatious whispers and sly glances, stopping at a secluded table in the back corner of the restaurant. It's illuminated only by soft candlelight casting a flickering glow.

"I've heard about this place," Parker states once we're seated and the hostess has left. "You'd think living an hour away, I'd have checked it out by now. But this is the busiest time of year for me, so it's hard to get away."

"You got away tonight," I remind her.

"That's different."

"How so?"

"Because this is a business meeting."

"So you only leave Holley Ridge if it's work-related?"

She shrugs. "I guess."

"Or maybe it's because you don't like giving up control," I remark.

She opens her mouth, a protest on the tip of her tongue.

"It's okay," I interject. "I'm the same way. Occupational hazard, I suppose. It's difficult to let go of certain things, especially when you run your own business."

She lifts her lips into a flirtatious smirk. "And I thought we were nothing alike, Mr. Grinch."

"Are you still calling me that because I pointed out how commercialized Christmas has become?"

"Also because you're trying to destroy Christmas for the entire town by buying Holley Ridge."

I start to remind her it's better than risking it going to auction, but before I can, a server approaches. Once we place our orders, she disappears, and I direct my stare at Parker, the candle on the table reflecting in her brilliant blue eyes.

She seems much more relaxed than during any of our previous encounters. It could be because she's able to enjoy a few hours to herself. I'd like to think my presence has played a part, too.

"So why is Holley Ridge so special?" I ask as she takes a sip from her glass of water.

She places it back on the table, then smooths a hand down the front of her dress. The motion causes the material around her chest to tighten, drawing my attention that way.

Which is the last thing I need right now.

It takes a Herculean effort on my part to keep my gaze locked with hers and refrain from ogling her body.

Or mentally undressing her.

Who am I kidding?

I've *already* mentally undressed her more times than I care to admit.

"You've seen for yourself how much people love it. The joy on their faces as they walk through the property and see all the twinkling lights. Or go for a horse-drawn carriage ride. Or ice skate."

"That's true. But I didn't ask what makes it special for everyone else." I lean toward her. "I want to know what makes it special for *you*. And not just because it's been in your family for generations. I could be wrong, but I sense this attachment goes deeper than that. It—"

"Here we are, sir," our server interrupts yet again with the bottle of wine Parker recommended, something from one of the vineyards in Sycamore Falls. After the server pours a little into my glass, I taste it.

I'm pleasantly surprised by the flavor of the Cabernet Sauvignon. It easily holds its own against many of the finer wines from Napa Valley.

"To impromptu business meetings." I raise my glass toward Parker once we're alone.

"To impromptu business meetings."

We clink glasses and I watch as she sips on her wine, swirling it around her mouth.

I've never wanted to be an inanimate object as much as I'd give anything to be that glass.

"Tell me," I press once she's had a chance to enjoy her wine. "Why is Holley Ridge special to you? What's one of your favorite memories?"

She pulls her bottom lip between her teeth. Her uncertainty surprises me. I assumed she'd regale me with a list of memories of her childhood home.

She takes another long sip of her wine, as if needing the liquid courage for whatever she's about to tell me. Then she lifts her gaze to mine. "My favorite memory is probably the first time I was there."

"What do you mean by that?" I straighten, confused. "I thought it's been in your family for generations."

"It has been. But my first time at Holley Ridge was at the kid's carnival, like the one you helped out at today."

I blink, her statement not making any sense. I reviewed the deed on the property before making an offer to make sure the title was clear. Her parents owned it. It's been in her family for generations. How could her first time on the property have been at the kid's carnival?

And then it hits me.

"You were in the foster care system," I exhale.

It all makes sense now, especially after hearing the determination in her voice earlier today as she spoke about doing everything to make sure foster kids believe in the magic of Christmas.

"My birth parents died when I was young. Only three." She gives me a tight-lipped smile, her eyes glossing over.

"Parker, I—"

"That first year, I remember looking forward to Christmas so damn much. My parents always made it so special. They didn't have a lot of money, but unlike you tend to believe…" She levels me with a pointed glare. "It wasn't about spoiling me with gifts. They still made it special without spending a fortune. We'd drive around to look at pretty holiday lights. Go to parks and play in the snow. Bake cookies together. I don't have a lot of memories of my birth parents anymore, but I still remember how loving they were."

She forces a smile, but I can tell it's pained. That she's not only remembering the happy times she spent with her parents but also that she lost them. Something I can't fathom, especially at such a young age.

"I'm so sorry, Parker." I shake my head. "I didn't know. I…" I trail off, not sure what to say.

Anything I *do* say is going to be grossly inadequate compared to this kind of loss. I may not have the best relationship with my family, especially my brother, but at least they're still alive.

"Truce?" She extends her hand toward me.

"Is that going to be our thing whenever one of us says something we regret?"

She shrugs. "It's better than holding a grudge. Don't you think?"

I can't help but admire her. Despite everything she endured as a young child, she's still so damn optimistic. Never complaining. Always positive.

The world could use more people like Parker Holley.

"Truce." The corners of my mouth tug up as I grasp her hand.

But instead of releasing her after we shake, I keep her hand enclosed in mine as I set it on the table. To my surprise, she doesn't pull away, even as my thumb grazes her knuckles.

"Santa never came the first year I was in foster care," she continues. "Or the second. Or the third. After the fourth, I sort of gave up hope. Stopped believing in Santa. Until the next year when the family I was with took me to Holley Ridge for a carnival they put on for foster kids. It was the first time I felt happy in ages. Seeing Santa. Opening presents. I actually smiled."

"How did you end up getting adopted?"

"My adoptive parents weren't able to have kids, so they tried to fill that void in other ways. Mama believed it was fate that brought us together. At the kid's carnival that year, they learned my current foster family would be relocating because of my foster father's job. The Holleys had been going through the adoption process for a while, but things kept falling through. They were about to give up since they were both nearing fifty. Luckily, they were already approved as foster parents, so they asked the state if they could be my new placement. My case worker agreed, and I moved in with them right before Christmas. A few years later, my adoption was finalized, and I officially became a Holley."

"They sound like incredible people."

"They were the best people," she says without hesitation, the respect and love she has for them obvious.

Our server reappears with our meals, breaking the moment. When Parker pulls her hand from mine, a chill sweeps over my skin from the loss of contact.

If nothing else comes out of tonight, at least it's allowed me to see Parker Holley in a different light. Understand what makes her tick a little better.

"I know selling is the smart thing," Parker says

after several long moments, both of us having taken a break in the conversation to enjoy our meals. Braised lamb for me. Salmon for her.

"It is?" I arch a brow.

"Like you said, if the property goes to auction, there's a chance I may not see even a fraction of what you're offering. May walk away worse off than I am now. But it's not just a piece of property to me. My parents did so much. Gave me a home. A family." She swallows hard.

"I feel like if I give up now, I'm giving up on them. That I'm letting go of them. They wouldn't have wanted me to get rich off selling the property to some real estate developer so he could build luxury homes on it. Their dream was to host weddings on that property. To see me get married in that barn. I can't give up on their dream now."

I take a large swallow of wine, then slice into the lamb again. "What if we come up with something different to do with the property? Something other than timeshares, since it seems readily apparent you hate that idea. If we came up with something that allows their dreams of hosting weddings to still be realized, would you be interested in selling then?"

She narrows her gaze on me. "We both know once I sign those papers and the property transfer goes through, you could change your mind, especially since the county zoning commission loves the idea of building as many condos and timeshares in the area as possible to increase tourism."

"That's true. But what if I give you my word we wouldn't destroy what you built? What your parents built? We could keep the barn and the inn. Maybe turn the property into more of a resort instead of impersonal condos and timeshares. I've been doing some research."

"You have?"

I nod.

"And I assumed you spent most of the day playing chess with your new friends."

"Have you been keeping tabs on me, Ms. Holley?"

A blush blooms on her cheeks. "Just making sure the resident grump doesn't do anything to ruin Christmas for others."

"Of course." Warmth fills me over the idea that she's been watching me.

Just like I've been watching her every chance I got over the past few days.

"Most of the surrounding towns are inundated with condos for all the snow bunnies," I continue. "My job entails not just finding a great piece of property to develop, but also determining gaps in the market that need to be filled. A resort could do that. And it won't be timeshares or condos."

She rubs her lips together, considering my

proposal. Then she pushes out a long sigh, making me think that's not good enough for her, either.

"I appreciate that you're willing to address my concerns. Or at least listen to them. I don't know if I can give you the answer you want, no matter what plans you come up with. Not when there's still a chance for a miracle. My parents didn't give up on their hope of adopting a child. I didn't give up on my hope of finally having a family again, although I was damn close. I can't give up on this. Not yet. Like I've told Haley and Estelle. If there's any time of year a miracle could happen, it's Christmas. So if you don't mind, I'd like to table this discussion until after Christmas. At that point, I'm more than happy to discuss this. Not until then."

I exhale a deep breath and nod. If she told me the same thing a week ago, I would have berated her for holding onto something as ridiculous as hope. Hell, I *did* berate her for thinking the universe would present her with a solution simply because she manifested one. Now that I've spent some time with her, I understand her a little better.

And not giving up hope is the most important thing to her.

For a few years, hope was all she had.

"Well then…" I grab my wine glass and raise it. "To Christmas miracles. I hope yours comes true."

"Even though it would mean you'd miss out on making millions of dollars?"

"Yes, Parker. Even though I'd miss out on making a lot of money."

She studies me for a beat, as if unsure whether I'm being sincere.

I can't quite explain it, but a part of me wants her to succeed. Wants her to save Holley Ridge. Wants her to receive this Christmas miracle.

Regardless of what it means for my firm's bottom line.

Finally, she lifts her glass and clinks it against mine. "To Christmas miracles."

FOURTEEN

Parker

"I guess it's time to get you back to Holley Ridge before you turn into a pumpkin," Callum remarks as he helps me into my coat after a longer than expected dinner.

Even once we finished our main courses, neither of us seemed ready to leave, so we stayed for dessert and coffee. And more coffee. And even more coffee.

Through it all, Callum didn't once bring up the possibility of buying Holley Ridge. Once I told him I wouldn't consider any offer until after Christmas, he stopped pressuring me. That meant more than his willingness to compromise on his plans for the property.

Callum places his hand on my lower back as he

leads me through the lobby of the hotel where the restaurant is located, holding the door open as we step out into the chilly night air.

But unlike when we were last outside, it's now snowing.

And quite heavily.

"Where did this come from?" Callum frowns as he surveys the snowflakes falling in the dark sky, the streets and buildings draped in white.

"That's winter in the mountains for you." I shrug. "It can come out of nowhere. And just because it's a clear forecast in Sycamore Falls doesn't mean it will be in these mountain towns that are at a higher elevation."

He faces me. "What should we do?"

I chew on my bottom lip, debating our options. I may have spent most of my life living in an area that gets frequent snow. I still hate driving in it, the roads slick and visibility limited.

At the same time, I hate the idea of being gone from Holley Ridge longer than necessary. Since I opened the inn, I haven't spent a single night away.

But I'd rather Callum not have to drive sixty miles in this weather. He seemed to be a safe driver on the ride up here. It's not him I'm worried about, though. It's all the other drivers on the road.

Pushing out a long sigh, I lift my eyes toward his. "We should probably play it safe and stay here for the night. It's coming down pretty hard. It's all winding mountain roads on the way home. Plus, if you don't have four-wheel drive or chains for your tires, highway patrol won't let you past the first checkpoint."

"It's a rental so I doubt it." He nods toward the front doors of the hotel. "Should we see if they have a couple of rooms available?"

"Sure."

Callum holds the door for me, a wall of warm air hitting us the second we step back inside.

"How can I help you this evening?" a chipper woman in her thirties asks as we approach the front desk.

"I was wondering if you have any rooms available," Callum says evenly. "We came up for dinner and didn't anticipate getting stuck in a snow storm."

"This certainly came out of nowhere, didn't it? Living in the mountains is always an adventure." She types on her keyboard for a few moments. "It looks like you're in luck, though. We do have a deluxe room available."

"Do you have two?"

"Sorry. Just the one. It's a busy time of year for us, as you can see." She gestures around the lobby, dozens of people milling about, taking in the decorations and ambience.

"Are there two beds at least?" Callum asks.

When her expression falls again, I know there's only one bed.

"Sorry. It's a deluxe king."

Callum turns toward me. "We can check somewhere else. See if another hotel in the area has two rooms. Or at least a room with separate beds."

I'm on the verge of agreeing. But how many hotels could this small town actually have? This is a guaranteed room. I'd hate to pass on it, only to be unable to find anywhere to stay. Plus, this is a really nice hotel. Marble floors. A cozy fireplace. And the Christmas tree is one of the most beautiful trees I've seen in a while.

Except for the ones on my property.

I'll always be partial to those.

"Let's just stay here. That way we're not driving around in the snow."

"If you're sure…" He arches a brow.

"It's not a big deal," I insist, although the idea of not just sharing a room with Callum but also a bed has me more nervous that I've been in a while.

Reaching into my purse, I grab my wallet and place my credit card onto the counter at the same time as Callum does.

"I've got it, Parker." He slides my card toward me.

"But you paid for dinner." I push my card toward the clerk once more.

"This is a business expense for me," he insists.

"Me, too," I remind him.

"True. But if you let me pay, you'll be sticking it to the man trying to buy your property." He leans toward me, dropping his voice to a low whisper. "If you're getting fucked anyway, may as well get something in return." He pulls back, his sinful eyes locking with mine. "Isn't that what Estelle told you?"

I try not to focus on the way my body reacts to hearing Callum say fuck. But my god, it's sexy as hell.

Then again, he could probably read my grocery list and I'd find it sexy as hell in his deep, gravelly voice.

"More or less."

"Then let me pay."

With a devious grin, I face the clerk. "You wouldn't happen to have a presidential suite we can upgrade to, would you? Something ridiculously expensive?"

Callum throws his head back and laughs, the sound echoing through the lobby. I don't think I'll ever get tired of hearing him laugh. Seeing him smile. For those few seconds, he's able to drop all pretenses and just relax.

He should do it more often.

"Sorry," the clerk says with a slight chuckle of her own. "But there *is* a mini bar in the room you can pillage."

"Works for me."

She takes Callum's credit card and swipes it. Once she's finished, she hands him an envelope with our keys, along with a bag of complimentary toiletries, such as a few toothbrushes and toothpaste, then directs us toward an elevator.

"After you," Callum offers once it arrives and the doors open.

He places his arm over the door, preventing it from closing on us, and I step inside, my body brushing his as I do. Then he joins me, making the small space feel even more miniscule.

The instant the door closes, my anxiety spikes, my heart pounding so fast I'm confident it's about to burst out of my chest. It's not the first time I've been alone with Callum. But it's the first time I've felt his presence to this extent. Felt this strange spark mounting with every second.

I'm hyper aware of every swipe of his tongue along his lips. Every subtle rise of his shoulders. Every glance he steals my way. The sooner I get out of this elevator, the better.

Although, I have a feeling being alone in a hotel room with him won't be any better.

When I don't think I can handle the electricity vibrating between us a moment longer, the doors open. I rush off the elevator as if I'm being chased by a serial killer.

If Callum finds my behavior strange, he doesn't

say anything, maintaining a comfortable distance as we walk down the carpeted hallway.

With every step we take, the more I begin to regret my decision to stay here. I should have run a quick search to see if there were any other hotels with availability, even if it's some cheap motel with rooms that reek of stale smoke. Anything other than a gorgeous hotel that screams sophistication and romance.

As we approach our room, Callum unlocks the door and holds it open, allowing me to enter in front of him, my surroundings just as luxurious as I imagined they would be.

My eyes fixate on the king-size bed with its pristine white duvet and fluffy pillows, and images of my body tangled with Callum's fill my head.

His rough hands exploring every inch of me.

His unshaven jawline scraping on my thighs.

His strong physique pressing me into the mattress as he thrusts in and out, giving me more pleasure than I've experienced in years.

"You okay?" His voice cuts through my fantasies, reminding me of his presence.

As if I need a reminder.

"Of course." I whirl around, attempting to pull myself together.

The way he looks at me makes that damn near impossible, especially when I notice him glance at my chest and lick his lips before returning his eyes to mine. It's obvious he's struggling with whatever this is between us as much as I am. It's just a matter of who's going to break first.

"Do you want to go to the bar?" I ask quickly, moving as far away from him and the bed as I can. "I could use a drink. Would you like a drink? I could use a drink."

"Could you now?" he retorts, obviously amused by my nervous rambling.

I draw in a deep breath in an attempt to settle my nerves, although I doubt even the most calming of breathing exercises will help subdue the butterflies flapping their wings in my stomach.

Or the fact that my libido is currently doing a series of stretches, assuming she'll finally get the release she's been craving.

"Since we can't get back to Sycamore Falls tonight, I may as well take advantage of my time here and check out their bar. Do some research on how I can improve my offerings at Holley Ridge next year."

"Of course. For research," he replies, not bringing up the fact that he'll most likely own the property next year.

"Exactly." I hold my head high, shoulders squared. "For research."

"Then, let's go research, Parker."

FIFTEEN

Callum

Thank God Parker asked to go to the bar.

Since learning we'll be sharing a room with just one bed, I've been desperate for something to help me relax. As it was, that elevator ride nearly killed me. It took every ounce of resolve I possessed not to push her against the wall and finally taste those lips I've been fantasizing about since I first laid eyes on her.

But the second I walked into that room, my fantasies became even more erotic, filled with all the things I'd love to do to Parker in that luxurious bed. All the pleasure I'd love to rip from her.

I needed to get out of there before I did something I'd regret. Before I crossed the line that's become more blurry with every passing day.

One thing is certain. Tonight is going to be a test of willpower.

One I may not pass.

Thankfully, this bar has a great selection of scotch to settle my nerves. And the wine has helped Parker relax, too. She's shared more memories of growing up at Holley Ridge and her relationship with Grandma Estelle, who I've learned technically isn't even a grandmother. Everyone in town simply calls her that because she's become a fixture at Holley Ridge, having taught many of the locals how to ride a horse.

I knew she was rather eccentric, but some of the stories Parker has shared have made my stomach hurt from laughing so much, especially when I learned of Grandma Estelle's unique taste in books, including alien and monster erotica.

"So tell me about you," Parker says after a while. "I've been blabbering on about myself. I've barely let you say more than a few words."

"I don't mind." I lift my glass to my mouth and take a small sip. "I like listening to you talk."

And watching her mouth move.

And imagining those bright red lips moving over other parts of my body.

But I can't exactly tell her that.

Although, if I have a few more drinks, I just might.

Maybe coming to the bar was a bad idea.

"I'm sure your life is much more interesting than mine," I tell her.

"My life's not that interesting. Hell, tonight's the first one I've spent away from Sycamore Falls since I opened the inn." She angles toward me in her barstool, the movement causing her knee to brush against mine.

It shouldn't cause this kind of reaction inside of me, but I can't ignore the jolt of electricity from the brief touching of our bodies, a spark igniting deep in my soul. I haven't felt this way around another woman in years. I didn't think I ever would again.

"What do you want to know?" I clear my throat.

Normally, I don't like talking about myself. Like I told her, my life isn't that interesting. Sure, I travel a lot. In the past year, I can count on one hand the number of weeks I've actually spent in my San Francisco apartment. I like being able to see the world, find properties that can make Daniel and me even richer.

"How old were you when you first kissed a girl?" Parker asks after a protracted pause.

"*That's* what you want to know?"

"Just trying to figure you out. What makes you tick." She inhales a sharp breath, eyes widening.

"Unless your first kiss was with a boy. I didn't mean to assume. I'm not judging. If you ask me, love is love."

Despite every voice in my head warning me this is a bad idea, I lean toward her, surrounding myself in her addictive scent of apples and cinnamon.

"All of my kisses have been with women, Ms. Holley," I say in a low voice, lingering for several protracted seconds, my gaze falling to the vein throbbing in her neck. What I wouldn't give to drag my tongue along her throat, dig my teeth into her flesh, feel her tremble against me, leaving her completely breathless.

I pull back to observe the effect I have on her. Her breathing grows more uneven, her lips parting as she squirms in her seat, uncrossing and re-crossing her legs.

Which only brings my attention to them.

"Sadie O'Connor," I announce, taking a big swallow of my drink.

Truthfully, I'm surprised I answered her. Then again, I need to do something to stop myself from thinking about Parker's legs. Still, saying that name doesn't hurt as much as I thought it would.

"What's that?" she replies breathlessly.

"My first real kiss was Sadie O'Connor. I passed her a note during fourth period English in seventh grade asking if she'd be my girlfriend. When she agreed, I told her I was going to kiss her on Friday after we got off the bus. She lived right next door to me."

"So you were the boy next door." She playfully waggles her brows.

"I was the boy next door," I repeat with a grin.

"And you scheduled your first kiss?"

"What can I say?" I shrug. "I've always been a planner. But Sadie was definitely more spontaneous." A nostalgic smile tugs on my lips. "You remind me of her in that respect. She'd probably do what you're doing. Would try to manifest a solution to her problem."

"I think I like this Sadie," Parker remarks, taking another sip from her glass.

I swallow hard, biting back my remark that she probably wouldn't if she knew the entire story.

"After I told her of my intentions," I continue, pushing down the memory of how everything fell apart, "she grabbed my cheeks and asked why I wanted to wait because she didn't. She kissed me right there in the school hallway, which was a big no-no and landed us both in detention for the entire week."

Parker throws her head back and laughs. "That's a great story."

I nod, neither agreeing nor disagreeing. It *is* a great story. One I'd hoped to be able to share with our children one day.

Too bad it didn't end like I'd hoped.

"So what about you? Who was the first boy you kissed?" I ask, even though the idea of anyone kissing her makes me oddly jealous. I just need to think about something other than my first kiss. My first everything, really.

"I like women," she deadpans.

"Oh." I straighten. "Okay. I mean, that's cool. I just—"

"I'm fucking with you." She gently shoves me. "Granted, I can definitely see the attraction in not dealing with men. Some of you act like children. But, for the most part, I like what your gender has to offer."

"Duly noted."

"My first kiss was John Tyler. He didn't schedule it with me. It just happened while we were at laser tag."

"Laser tag?"

"Don't tell me you never went to laser tag when you were a teenager. Where you wear those silly vests and go around with a laser gun pretending to kill people."

"I know what laser tag is. I was quite skilled at it."

"John and I were on the same team and were hiding behind one of the pillars in the arena. The rest of our team was already out, and the other team was closing in on us, so it was only a matter of time before we were 'killed', too.

"As we were huddled together, he told me he

didn't want to die without kissing a girl. He was really playing up the dramatics of the game. I had to give him points for the amount of effort he exhibited just to kiss me. So I went along with it. Of course, while we were kissing, the other team eliminated us. But it didn't matter. It was a memorable first kiss, even if it wasn't great. I doubt anyone's first kiss is the type Grandma Estelle reads about in her monster erotica."

I chuckle, taking another drink from my glass. "I'll never look at her the same way again."

"Glad I could make your stay at the Inn at Holley Ridge a memorable one."

"More than you'll ever know," I respond softly, my eyes locking with hers.

In a heartbeat, the atmosphere shifts from light and playful to something else. Something heavy.

She darts out her tongue and licks her lips, drawing my eyes to her mouth, her chest rising and falling in a quicker pattern.

The air crackles between us, and I curve toward her, my pulse slowly increasing with each inch I erase.

Just when I can all but taste her lips on mine, she abruptly pulls back and jumps down from her barstool.

"I...," she stammers, her complexion flushed as she averts her gaze. Then she draws in a deep breath. "I need to use the ladies' room. I'll be right back."

I squeeze my eyes shut, cursing myself for what I was about to do.

What was I thinking? Parker has bad idea written all over her. It's one thing to hook up with a woman I meet in a hotel bar when I'm scouting properties or overseeing development.

It's another to hook up with the woman whose property I'm trying to buy.

"Do you want another?" I gesture to her empty wine glass.

She bites on her bottom lip. "Probably not a good idea."

"Right. Of course. I'll settle up and meet you in the lobby."

"Sounds good."

I watch as she walks away, unable to stop looking at her. Even when she catches me unabashedly checking her out, I still don't stop. I expect her to shoot daggers at me, or give me some sort of look of disapproval.

Instead, as she continues toward the lobby, she sways her hips a little more, glancing over her shoulder and winking before disappearing from view.

It's official. If I'm to spend the night in the same room as her, I'm going to need a cold shower.

I signal the bartender and ask for the check, draining the rest of my scotch. After charging our drinks to the room and leaving a generous cash tip, I head out to the lobby.

As I'm waiting, I notice a gift shop with an assortment of souvenirs, including Christmas pajamas. Figuring we'll both be more comfortable sleeping in something other than our clothes, I slip inside and grab a set for Parker, as well as a pair of snowman boxer shorts for me, returning to the lobby just as she rounds the corner.

"Buying more souvenirs?"

"Figured you might like some pajamas to sleep in."

"Probably a good idea." A devilish glint sparkles in her eyes as she steps closer, barely a breath separating us. "Otherwise, I'd be forced to sleep in just my bra and panties." Her eyes drift up to meet mine, her voice growing sultry. "And we wouldn't want that. Now would we?"

"Parker," I growl through a clenched jaw. I'm trying so hard not to cross that line between us.

But before I can say anything else, a familiar voice cuts through. "Callum?"

I freeze, my heart dropping to pit of my stomach.

For a moment, I give serious contemplation to ignoring it and whisking Parker away to our room. But when I notice the expression on Parker's face as she looks between me and the man standing only a few feet behind me, I know I can't pretend I don't know him.

It's kind of hard to act like you don't know someone who's a carbon copy of you and knows your name.

Slowly turning around, I look into my brother's eyes for the first time in three years. Just my luck, *she's* with him, too. Why wouldn't she be? After all, she married him.

"Hello, Mason," I say evenly, his name leaving a sour taste in my mouth.

"What are you doing here?"

"We came for dinner and got stuck because of the snow." I straighten my tie as I glance at Parker.

"This is Parker Holley. Parker, this is my brother, Mason, and his wife…" I swallow hard as my eyes lock on hers, then finish, "Sadie."

SIXTEEN

Parker

I blink repeatedly, struggling to form a coherent thought. And not simply because I'm staring at a near mirror image of Callum, minus the suit and perfectly groomed hair. This guy is definitely a bit more rugged.

It's that name.

Sadie.

If it were something like Mary or Jennifer, I wouldn't have batted an eye. But Sadie? There's no doubt in my mind this is the same Sadie he just told me about.

The same Sadie who was his first kiss.

And now she's married to Callum's brother.

But not just any brother.

His twin brother.

His *identical* twin brother.

Is Sadie the reason Callum closed up during dance lessons? Were they supposed to get married and she called it off at the last minute, as I'd joked?

Based on the tension crackling between Sadie, Mason, and Callum, I get the feeling something like that happened.

I can't even imagine how much that must have hurt Callum. I can understand why he'd be so closed off and cold. If someone I trusted went behind my back and engaged in any kind of relationship with someone I loved, I'd be bitter, too. Would have trouble trusting again.

"Nice to meet you, Parker." Mason extends his hand toward me.

"You, too." I shake his hand, then glance toward Sadie, her expression wide and nervous. I push down the pang of jealousy bubbling inside me over the idea that this woman once knew Callum intimately.

"Mom's been trying to reach you," Mason tells Callum.

"I've been busy."

"She misses you, Cal." He steps toward him. "We all do. You should come this year for Christmas. Meet little Levi. I'd like for him to know his uncle."

I didn't think my heart could ache any more for Callum.

I was wrong.

Not only did this woman Callum cared deeply for marry his brother, but they also have a kid?

I may have been in my fair share of relationships that ended badly, but none of them were as horrible as this.

"I'll think about it," Callum says in a low voice that lacks all emotion. "If you'll excuse us."

He places his hand on the small of my back and leads me toward the elevators. No goodbye. No nice to see you. No acknowledgment of these two people who were once important to him.

"It was good seeing you, Cal," Mason calls after him, but he doesn't stop, his steps quickening instead. "And great meeting you, Parker."

I glance over my shoulder and give him a small smile. Callum keeps his gaze forward, eyes hardened, muscles tense. I want to say something. But what can I say that will make this sting less?

After one of the most uncomfortable elevator rides of my life, we walk silently down the hallway. Like before, Callum's the perfect gentleman, holding the door for me. Once we're inside, he hands me one of the bags from the gift shop, his expression impassive.

I duck into the bathroom and quickly change into a cute set of snowman pajama bottoms and a t-shirt. After folding my bra and panties and returning them to the bag, I splash some water onto my face, scrubbing off my makeup.

When I slip back into the room, Callum doesn't even look at me, grabbing his own bag and disappearing into the bathroom. I'd almost rather have the sexual tension back from earlier. It would be preferable to this.

While I've never been one to solve my problems with alcohol, I think running into your ex who left you and is now married to and has a child with your twin brother qualifies as an exception.

I walk over to the mini bar and survey its contents, settling on whiskey. After pouring some into a glass, I open the refrigerator, finding some champagne.

At the sound of the bathroom door opening, I look up, resisting the urge to comment on Callum's snowman boxers with a giant carrot right where his dick is. Or ogle his bare chest, his chiseled muscles on full display, making my mouth water.

If circumstances were different, I absolutely would ogle.

Callum Reed without a shirt on is a glorious sight to behold, all defined abs and muscles, complete with a happy trail of hair disappearing into his shorts.

"Sorry about all of that," he says, forcing my eyes to his. They're the first words he's said to me since the lobby. "I didn't mean to involve you in family drama."

He runs a hand through his hair and pushes out a long sigh. It makes him look so vulnerable.

Completely unlike the man I assumed he was when we first met. I didn't think Callum Reed had a soft side. Or had feelings.

Again, I was wrong about him.

"It's okay."

"And in case you're wondering, because I'm sure it's killing you, yes. That's the same Sadie I told you about. The one I tried to schedule my first kiss with."

I approach him, handing him the glass of whiskey. He brings it up to his mouth and takes a long swallow as I sip on my champagne.

"We were married," he declares after a beat, lowering himself onto the edge of the mattress.

"Callum, I'm—"

"You were right last week. Kind of."

"About?" I sit on the bed, but keep some distance between us.

"Taking dance lessons for a wedding. I took them with her." He pulls his bottom lip between his teeth.

"We were high school sweethearts. But before that, we were friends. Best friends, really. Mason, too. The three of us were always together. When it came time to go to college, Sadie went to a different school. But Mason and I went to the same one."

He runs a hand down his face, taking a moment. I

don't push him to talk. Don't ask questions. Just let him share whatever he's comfortable with.

"Mom always joked we were born entrepreneurs. We were the kids who would try to upsell you a turkey dinner when all you wanted was a glass of water. When we were in college, we found a way to buy a three-family home across from campus. Fixed it up. Rented out the spare rooms. A year later, we sold it at a profit of over fifty grand."

I laugh slightly. "Sounds like real estate's always been in your blood."

"His, too. We started our first company when we were only twenty. We'd buy houses in horrible shape, fix them up, often living there as we renovated, then sell them at huge profits. I'd made my first million by the time I turned twenty-two."

"That's incredible," I exhale, in awe of his accomplishments.

"It was. And the first thing I did was ask Sadie to marry me. In retrospect, maybe we were too young, but I didn't care. I thought we'd be that couple who made it."

"What happened?"

"I saw the money people were making by developing real estate from the ground up. That's what I wanted to do. Instead of making ten or fifteen grand on a flip, we could make millions by developing unused land into subdivisions. So we started a second firm. A real estate development firm. Unfortunately, development isn't as easy as flipping. With bigger profit margins comes more responsibilities. More hours. But I loved it. Loved traveling and finding land to develop. It was such a rush. It still is."

He speaks with so much passion and zeal, his expression lighting up. As much as I've begrudged him for what he does, it's obvious he loves it.

"And Sadie?" I swallow hard. "How did she feel about all the hours you were working?"

"I think it's obvious." He stares ahead, taking another sip of his drink. "I thought we were happy. We saw so many of our friends struggling to make ends meet. Not Mason and me. Every year brought more and more success our way. Everything was going so great. And when I found that pregnancy test in the trash and Sadie confirmed it, I was over the moon. Every city I traveled to, I brought back something for our baby. Learning she was carrying our child, watching her belly grow every day… Words can't explain how I felt."

My heart squeezes listening to him talk about having a child. A week ago, I never would have imagined Callum the type of person to want children. He seemed too much of an ass. But now, hearing the joy in his voice, seeing the excitement on his face, it makes me jealous of Sadie.

And angry at her for destroying this version of Callum.

"And then I did the math." He throws back a hefty gulp of whiskey.

"Oh, god…"

"It took me a while. It was actually my current business partner, Daniel, who pointed it out to me. Got into a pretty big fight over it, too. I didn't want to think Sadie would cheat on me, though. I'm not proud of it, but I hired a private investigator to keep an eye on her while I was out of town. After a month, the PI told me he couldn't find any proof of infidelity. That the only person he saw her with was me. The only problem was that I hadn't been in town." His Adam's apple works in his throat, his voice strained. "But my brother was."

"Callum, I…" I shake my head. I don't even know what to say right now. How do you respond to a story of such immense betrayal?

"And the part that really gutted me was that she let me believe it was my child for over five months." His jaw ticks, the hand holding his glass tightening to the point I'm worried it'll shatter in his hand. "They both did. They knew. I wasn't supposed to find that pregnancy test. But since I did, they were just waiting for the right time to tell me."

"That's… That's just awful, Callum."

He nods, throwing back the rest of his whiskey.

"So there you have it. That's why I have no plans to go to Christmas at my mother's this year or any other year. Not when I'll be forced to sit there and watch the little boy I thought was mine call my twin brother Daddy."

Not caring about the consequences, I fling my arms around him, my champagne jostling slightly with my motions. But that's the least of my concerns right now.

I just want him to feel something other than the soul-crushing despair after enduring something so horrible.

Luckily, he doesn't push away. Just lets me hug him. To my surprise, he hugs me back in his own way, running his hand along my arm, his touch delicate, light.

But it still sends a shiver down my spine. Still has my pulse increasing.

And with each brush along my skin, his touch becomes more resolute. More determined. More sensual.

When his lips scrape against my neck, as if testing the waters, I lift my eyes to meet his. My heart pounds, my stomach doing somersaults. This man is temptation in human form.

And I'm trying so hard not to give in.

"Callum, I—" I begin, about to push away, but he doesn't let me, his grip on me tightening.

"Don't, Parker. Not tonight."

"Don't what?"

"Don't fight it," he pleads, his voice gruff but strained at the same time. "I know you feel this, too."

"Feel what?" I ask breathlessly.

"I don't even know. All I do know is I haven't been able to stop thinking about you for even a second since the day we met."

I should do something to break the spell he so easily cast over me. But the rational part of my brain has officially checked out, as is so often the case whenever Callum is near.

Now all I can think about is succumbing to these urges that have grown stronger every day.

"What have you thought about?"

A peaceful smile tugs on his lips, a noticeable shift from the despair that consumed him moments ago.

"Your positive attitude, as infuriating as it was in the beginning." He takes my glass from me, setting it along with his on the night stand. "Now that I know more about you, about your childhood, it makes sense." He cups my cheek, the roughness of his hand invigorating me. "Makes you even more remarkable, considering you didn't let everything you went through extinguish your light."

"What else?" I press, not wanting him to stop touching me. Not wanting whatever this is to be over just yet.

We're in a bubble. A snowed-in, one-bed bubble. And I want to enjoy every second of it.

"Your smile." His mouth curves up in the corners. "The way it made me feel again for the first time in ages. Made me smile again for the first time in ages, as much as I fought it at first."

"What else?" I ask again, my breathing growing ragged as I inch closer, barely a whisper separating us.

"Your lips." He runs the pad of his thumb along my bottom lip. It's a gentle touch, but it still lights me on fire, an inferno I doubt will ever be extinguished. "I couldn't stop wondering how they would taste. How they would feel."

I dart out my tongue, briefly swiping his thumb as I do.

"Then why don't you find out?"

A part of me expects some hesitation. For him to realize his need for me is probably just a consequence of seeing his ex with his brother after all this time.

But there isn't a hint of reluctance as he brings his free hand to my face in an unrelenting grip, his eyes darkening with hunger .

Then he slams his lips against mine.

SEVENTEEN

Parker

I don't care if this is a bad idea. Don't care if this won't lead to anything. Don't care if Callum Reed could very well destroy my heart.

Right now, none of that matters.

All that does is how fucking incredible his lips feel against mine.

He's gentle at first, his tongue exploring my mouth with the care of an archeologist hoping to discover something of importance.

That only lasts a matter of seconds before desperation takes over. A groan rumbles from his throat as he moves a hand to my waist and tugs me on top of him, my legs straddling him.

"Callum," I moan when his erection hits my center, my pajama bottoms an unwelcome barrier.

"This is what you do to me, Parker," he exhales as he shifts from my lips, peppering rough kisses down my throat. I crane my head, elongating my neck to give him better access. "What you've done to me since the day we met. There's just something about you that drives me absolutely crazy."

He digs his fingers into my hair, yanking my mouth back to his. We're all heavy breaths, desperate tongues, and clashing teeth. I circle my hips, my core throbbing as I rub myself against him. This insane need to feel every inch of him overtakes me, and I kiss him harder, pulsing faster.

With a lustful growl, he flips me onto my back in one swift move, my body bouncing from the impact.

"What's the matter?" I say coyly as he crawls between my legs. "Don't like a woman on top?"

He bites his bottom lip. "On the contrary, Ms. Holley..." His mouth comes within a breath of mine. "I quite like feeling you on top of me. Unfortunately, I liked it a little too much." He gives me a knowing look. "If you kept grinding on me like that, Frosty's carrot would have exploded."

I bark out a laugh, the sound echoing through the room. "I'll admit. The boxers are a big turn on."

"Do you only like me for my carrot?" He slowly pulses against me, and a subtle whimper escapes.

"Hard to say."

"How so?"

"Because I've never seen your…carrot."

He skims his lips against mine. "Do you want to?" His rhythm becomes more intense, teasing me to the point that I'm ready to lose my mind if I don't feel him inside me soon.

"God, yes." I throw my head back, losing myself in the sensation.

"I was hoping you'd say that. Because I really want to see your…" He trails off, lifting his gaze to meet mine. "You know what? I'm struggling to come up with a decent innuendo for pussy."

His eyes darken as he trails a hand down the curve of my frame, slipping it between my thighs and rubbing against me. There may be a thin layer of cotton between us, but there's no doubt he can feel how wet I am.

"But I really want to see your pussy."

I release a moan as he continues to tease me, desperate to rid myself of every scrap of clothing separating us.

"Really want to taste your pussy." He slams his mouth back against mine, his tongue plunging inside.

A kiss isn't supposed to be this explosive. This all-consuming. It's not supposed to make me feel like I'd physically ache without this man's lips on mine.

He brings our kiss to an end, straightening slightly

as he stops rubbing against me. Disappointment fills me from the lack of his touch. But it's short-lived when he teases his finger along the waistband of my pajama pants, the anticipation threatening to unravel me.

"But do you know what I really want to do?"

"What's that?" I pant.

His lips hover over mine as his hand disappears into my pants. When he slides a finger along my folds, I exhale a moan.

"Fuck, Parker. I really want to fuck this pussy." He slips a finger inside me, and I cry out in pleasure, squirming and writhing beneath him. "Want to feel your walls constrict around me. Want your cunt to milk me fucking dry."

"Holy shit," I exhale, barely able to put together a coherent thought. I wasn't sure what Callum would be like in the bedroom. Truthfully, I did my best *not* to think about it.

But damn if hearing him say these things doesn't turn me on even more. Makes me burn for him in a way I've never hungered for another person.

"Can I do that? Can I fuck you?"

"Yes, Callum."

I grab his face, circling my hips as I chase my orgasm, silencing the rational voice reminding me this is a horrible idea. That this won't end well. That doesn't matter right now. All that does is finally releasing this pent-up sexual tension that's been mounting for days.

"I need you." I urge his lips toward mine, but before I can lose myself in his kiss, he resists, staying just out of reach.

"Need what exactly? What do you need me to do?"

"Callum," I begin as evenly as possible in my current state. "I need you to fuck me."

He slams his lips against mine. "I fucking love your mouth." He slips his finger out of me and rips my shirt over my head. "Fucking love these tits." He cups my breasts, taking each nipple between his thumb and forefinger.

My eyes flutter shut, pinpricks of pleasure dancing over my skin. This entire scenario still feels surreal. Like I'll wake up any second and learn it was all a dream. An incredibly erotic dream, but a dream nonetheless.

Until Callum takes one of my nipples in his mouth, the warmth of his tongue lapping at the pert bud followed by the scraping of his teeth making it clear this is real.

"I need you," I whimper again, unsure how much more of this torturous foreplay I can take before I lose all damn control.

He travels down my body, scraping his scruff against my stomach, the roughness invigorating.

Electrifying.

Combustible.

"And you'll have me. But first…" He hooks his fingers into the waistband of my pajamas. I eagerly lift my hips off the bed in invitation. "I need to taste this pussy I've been desperate to bury my face in since I walked in on you talking about feeling my facial hair on your thighs."

I can't even pretend to be embarrassed about that now. Not when I'm on the brink of finally feeling his mouth on me.

"Can I do that?" He slides my pants down my legs and drops them onto the floor.

"God, yes," I moan as he returns to me, pushing my thighs wide.

My heart pounds a staccato rhythm, making me all but certain it's about to smash through the walls of my chest. With a sinful stare, he leisurely licks his lips, the promise of feeling that tongue on me making me squirm.

And he knows it. Knows this is absolute torture.

But when he drags his tongue along my center, releasing all the tension inside me, it's worth it. Because nothing has ever felt remotely close to this.

"So fucking delicious," he groans, lapping at my

clit as he teases my entrance with a finger. "So fucking wet." He slides a finger inside, and I pulse against him, desperate for more. "So fucking greedy."

When he adds another finger, stretching and massaging, sparks ignite deep in my core, my muscles tightening. I don't want to come yet. Want this to last.

But it's been so long since I've had a man between my thighs that I can't control how fast I reach that peak.

Or maybe it's because Callum seems to be able to play me like a skilled musician, knowing exactly what to say, where to touch me to make me sing.

"That's it, baby," he growls as I move against him, chasing that high. "Fuck my face. Rub your cunt all over me."

He adds one more finger as he nibbles on my clit, and that's all it takes for me to see stars, my body a slave to his expert touch.

"Callum!" I scream out, not even caring other guests may hear. That's the least of my concerns right now. All I do care about is prolonging this incredible sensation as long as possible.

And as Callum continues lapping at me, he seems to want that, too.

"So what's the verdict?" he asks as my tremors start to subside, my vision no longer a kaleidoscope of stars.

"Verdict?" I pant.

"Yeah." He treats me to a smile, my desire coating his lips. "Is the reality as good as the fantasy?"

I dig my fingers through his hair, forcing him up my body. "It's infinitely better." I slam my mouth against his, the taste of me on his tongue reigniting the flame that's barely had a chance to extinguish.

"And you're even more delicious than I've imagined."

"You've imagined?"

"Every night, Parker."

He slowly slides off me to stand, walking over to where he left his pants draped over the chair in the corner. Finding his wallet, he retrieves a condom before returning to me. When he pushes his shorts down his legs and his erection springs free, a thrill of anticipation spirals through me, which only increases when Callum rips open the packet and rolls the condom on his impressive length.

He crawls back onto the bed, settling between my legs once more. "Every night since we met, I've jerked off thinking about fucking you."

"Then why don't you find out if the real thing's as good as you imagined?"

"Gladly."

I expect him to immediately thrust inside. Instead, he teases me with his tip. I circle my hips, bracing to feel him push into me.

When he does, we both release a collective sigh. He's not harsh or forceful, easing inside inch by incredible inch, letting me get used to his size until he's fully seated.

"Fuck, Parker," he exhales, taking a moment to savor this amazing sensation. Then he covers my mouth, kissing me like I'm oxygen and he's struggling to breathe. "I could stay here forever. You're so soft." He pushes a tendril of hair out of my face. "So goddamn perfect."

"Please," I beg, desperate to feel some sort of friction. I wrap my legs around him.

"You want me to fuck you?"

"Need it."

He brushes a kiss to my lips. "I'll always give you everything you need, Ms. Holley."

He straightens, forcing me to release the hold my legs have on him. Then he slams into me, causing me to cry out.

"Like that?" he grunts, face scrunched tight with barely contained need. "Is that how you want it?"

I squeeze my eyes shut, overwhelmed with the things Callum makes me feel. "Yes."

He slowly retreats before thrusting into me once more, lingering for several moments, then pulling back again. This time when he drives into me, he doesn't pause. Doesn't stop. Just continues his relentless assault.

He covers my body with his, grabbing my hands and pinning them above my head. His mouth consumes me, the gentleness in the way his tongue slides against mine at complete odds with how roughly he pistons into me.

I wrap my legs back around his waist and he tears out of the kiss, struggling to catch his breath.

"I'm not going to last much longer," he confesses, the tension in his expression making it clear he's barely holding on.

"It's okay. Let go."

He shakes his head. "Not before I get one more out of you." He straightens, eyes locked on mine as he drags his tongue along his thumb. Then he presses it against my clit.

I moan, the sensation of his thumb on my clit and his cock moving inside me almost too much. "I don't think I can."

"You can. And you will. Stop thinking and just feel, Parker. Feel me."

"Oh, god," I whimper, climbing even higher.

"That's right. That's my girl."

I'm not sure if it's the way he moves inside me. Or how he leans forward and nibbles on my neck. Or hearing him call me his girl that does it. But in that moment, I lose all control, another orgasm ravaging through me, this one even more intense than the previous.

EIGHTEEN

Callum

Asliver of sunlight peeks through the shades, and I've never cursed morning as much as I do right now. I wanted the night to last forever. Wanted to keep Parker in my arms as long as possible.

Nothing's ever felt so right. So damn perfect.

If I'd run into my brother and Sadie any other time, I'm not sure I would have handled it as well as I did. I probably would have tossed and turned all night, wondering if there was something I could have done differently to prevent her from cheating on me, and with my own brother.

For months after I learned the truth, that's precisely what I did. Blamed myself. Because that's what Sadie and my brother did. They blamed me.

Said if I didn't work so much, Sadie wouldn't have felt so lonely.

It took me years to finally realize that was only something they said to make themselves feel better.

Once I kissed Parker, all thoughts of my brother and Sadie disappeared.

All thoughts of *work* have disappeared, too.

When I'm with Parker, she consumes me completely.

And I don't know how to feel about this.

Ever since I lost Sadie, I've lived my life with one singular focus — growing my firm into one of the most successful real estate development companies in the country, maybe even the world.

I love my work.

It's safe.

It's dependable.

It's something I can control.

At least more than I can control another person's emotions and feelings.

But now I feel like I'm losing all control. And I don't hate it.

Parker stirs in my arms, forcing me back to the present. When she rubs her ass against me, I'm powerless to resist her, my erection springing back to life.

"Down, boy," she remarks in a raspy voice.

I pull her closer, circling my hips. "I can't help it.

My cock has a mind of its own around you. Especially when you rub this amazing ass against him."

I run my hand along her side, relishing in the softness of her skin before traveling across her hipbone and toward the apex of her thighs. She eagerly parts them, just as desperate for my touch as I am to feel the most intimate parts of her body.

I bury my head in the crook of her neck, nipping on her flesh as I run my fingers through her heat. "Or this soaking wet cunt."

"Callum," she pants, slowly moving against me, telling me with her body how much she needs my touch. "You have a wicked mouth."

"From what I could tell last night, and the multiple times you crawled on top of me in the early morning hours, you quite enjoy my wicked mouth."

I push a finger inside her, and she whimpers. "Do I ever."

"Then I'd love to put my wicked mouth on you again. Feast on you until I've licked every last drop."

"That sounds like heaven." She circles against me with increasing need, greedily fucking my hand. One thing is certain. Parker has no problem going after what she wants.

And I'm more than happy to give it to her.

I'm about to push her onto her back, but before I can, she rolls over to face me, hooking a leg over my waist and forcing me onto my back.

"But first..." She straddles me, rubbing her slick pussy over my erection.

Her body is a goddamn masterpiece, especially as the early morning light hits her, accentuating the swell of her breasts and curve of her hips. Not to mention the look of pleasure on her face as she teases me.

She leans closer, her breath warm against my skin. "I want to put my wicked mouth on you." She arches a single brow. "Would you like that?"

I didn't think it was possible to get any harder than I already am, especially as she continues to rub herself on me.

I was wrong.

The mere idea of having Parker's lips wrapped around my dick, of coaxing her to relax her jaw as she takes every inch, causes electricity to rush through me, hunger and want colliding together in an addictive combination that has me forgetting all the reasons this is a bad idea.

"God yes," I moan.

"Your wish is my command, Mr. Reed."

She snakes down my body, peppering kisses along my chest and abs. When she reaches my waist, my pulse kicks up, eyes flaming as she wraps her fingers around my erection and gives it several slow jerks. I hold my breath, the seconds stretching as she parts her lips, slowly lowering her mouth toward me. Finally, she circles my tip with her tongue, and I release a low hiss, my muscles tightening, jaw clenching.

"Goddamn, baby," I groan, digging my fingers into her hair. "You're driving me crazy. You know that, right?"

"That's the plan." A coy smile tugs on her mouth. "Want to make you lose control."

"And I want to so damn badly. Want to lose control with you." My grip on her hair tightens. "So be a good girl and suck me off."

She moistens her lips, making my need for her increase even more. "Gladly."

I brace to feel her mouth around me, anticipation somersaulting inside me, each drawn out second lasting an eternity. Especially when she changes course, dragging her tongue along one side of my length, teasing my tip before continuing down the other side. It's fucking torture, and she knows it.

"Do you like being a tease?"

"I like knowing how desperate you are for me. Like seeing the effect I have on you."

I wrap her hair around my hand, holding her in place. "And I am. More so than anyone I've ever been with."

I don't know what causes me to say this. I normally don't share these kinds of thoughts or feelings with the women I sleep with.

Then again, Parker Holley isn't most women. She

never has been. I felt it that very first day, despite how infuriating I thought she was. And I worry I'll feel it even when I leave Sycamore Falls and go on with my life.

"You make me desperate for you, too." She inches her lips closer to my dick. "So damn desperate," she finishes as she finally takes me in her mouth.

I expel a sigh, basking in the sensations filling me as her warmth surrounds me, her hand still jerking me at the base. And like the greedy girl she is, she takes as much of me as she can, her tongue swirling as she moves her hand to cup my balls. When she releases my erection and drags her tongue along them, I groan, unsure how much longer I can last.

"Your mouth is goddamn dangerous, Parker."

She smirks, about to put her mouth back on me. But before she can, I yank her toward me, forcing her legs to straddle my waist.

"What are you doing? I told you I wanted to taste you."

"And you did." I move a hand to her center, toying with her clit. "But I need to be inside you. Can I do that?"

"Yes, Callum," she whimpers as she grinds against me.

"There's just one problem."

She stops, her mouth turning into a frown. "What's that?"

"I'm out of condoms." I grimace, but quickly add, "If you're concerned about pregnancy, you don't have to be. I had a vasectomy several years ago."

Her expression falls slightly. "You did?"

"After Sadie, I didn't want to put myself through that again."

She doesn't say anything for several moments. Just stares ahead, processing this. Finally, she brings her mouth toward mine. "Then what are you waiting for?"

"Are you sure? I can run to a convenience store if you'd prefer."

She wraps her hand around my erection once more and brings it up to her center, teasing me with her warmth. "I'm sure."

I cup her cheek, my fingers digging into her skin. "Then ride me, baby."

She doesn't need me to ask twice. She eases onto me, each inch she takes making my hunger for her grow.

I didn't think it was possible for sex to feel even more incredible than it did the multiple times I buried myself inside her throughout the night.

But being inside Parker with no barrier is more electrifying. More invigorating. Just...more.

"Goddamn," I grunt, my breaths coming fast and heavy.

"So deep," she exhales, eyes fluttering closed as her lips part.

I grip her hips and guide her, needing the friction of her sliding up and down my length. After a few seconds, she takes over, circling against me with determination, chasing her pleasure.

When she cups her breasts and pinches her nipples, I nearly lose control. It's so damn erotic. So damn intoxicating.

As if watching her play with her breasts wasn't enough of a turn on, she snakes a hand down her stomach, eyes locking with mine as she rubs her clit.

"Is that what you like, Parker? Like my dick inside you while you touch yourself?"

"Yes." She increases her motions, fucking me with more ferocity as she moves her fingers over herself even harder.

"That's it, baby. Get yourself off. Come all over my dick. Let me feel your pussy clench."

"Callum!" she exclaims, her body convulsing as she unravels around me.

I don't wait for her to come down, tossing her off me and propping her up on her hands in knees before slamming into her.

She buries her head into the pillow, muffling her screams as I relentlessly drive into her, each thrust propelling me higher than the last until I let out a strangled cry and pull out of her, releasing all over her ass and back.

"Holy fuck," she exhales, her legs shaking.

"You've got that right." I loop my arm around her waist, helping to lower her onto the mattress. Then I grab the towel off the floor before returning to her.

"I almost don't want to clean you up," I say, wiping my cum off her. "I like having my scent on your skin." I lean down, nipping at her neck. "Like knowing I've marked you."

"How very caveman of you." She shifts her head to the side, meeting my gaze.

"I can't help it around you. You bring out this side of me I didn't..." I trail off, not wanting to involve feelings. Not when they don't matter. They can't matter. I won't let them matter. I learned that lesson the last time.

"Well, you turn me into an animal, Parker."

I toss the towel onto the floor, then crawl beside her. Pulling her into my embrace, I savor in the warmth of her fingers as they trace circles around my chest.

"I could get used to this," she murmurs.

"What? Snuggling?"

"No. Getting fucked so good I see stars."

I throw my head back and laugh. "Glad I could satisfy you." I press a kiss to her temple, a comfortable silence falling between us. Probably because neither one of us wants to address the fact it's daytime and the roads are now clear, allowing us to return to the real world.

"But I also really like snuggling with you, too," she adds. "Like feeling your arms around me."

A voice in my head tells me to use this opportunity to redraw the lines. Tell her this is all there can ever be between us. That I'm not the marrying or even the relationship type. Not anymore. Not after Sadie.

But I don't want to burst our bubble just yet.

Instead, I pull her closer and breathe her in. "Me, too."

NINETEEN

Parker

A flash of auburn hair barrels toward me as I walk through the Christmas market, barely able to brace myself before Haley all but assaults me.

"How was it? Tell me everything. Why the hell didn't you respond to any of my texts? You know it's been killing me."

"I have a business to run, in case you haven't noticed." I stroll past all the vendors, happy to have such a large turnout on a Thursday evening. Typically, I don't see crowds this size until the weekend.

"I understand that, but you can't leave a girl hanging. Especially since that man looked like he was getting ready to rip off your dress last night when you left on your date."

"It was not a date." I roll my eyes, fighting against the grin wanting to break free from the memory of just how incredible my not-date was.

"Then why did you stay out all night?" She playfully nudges me. "According to Mabel Green, who heard from Claire, you called after ten last night to say you wouldn't be back until tomorrow. Well, today. When I stopped by the café this morning to grab a cup of coffee, everyone was talking about it. Then when I took some of the dogs to the off-leash park earlier, everyone I saw drilled me to find out what I knew about Parker's new man."

I groan, cursing under my breath.

I shouldn't be surprised by this. Small town gossip is alive and well, especially in Sycamore Falls. I have no doubt by tomorrow morning, I'll be pregnant with his child.

In rumor only, of course.

Because that's not possible. Not when he got a vasectomy.

Knowing he went to those extremes to protect himself after what Sadie and his brother did still squeezes my heart. I can't even imagine going through something so heartbreaking. Getting excited for a baby, only to learn it's not yours.

No wonder he's an emotional island.

"We got stuck in a snowstorm."

"So you didn't have a sleepover?" She arches a disbelieving brow as we approach the ice skating rink.

"Not like that," I insist.

Even though it kind of was.

"He took me up to Lyden Springs, but it started snowing pretty heavily. Instead of driving in those conditions, we stayed over."

She faces me, clasping her hands together. "Please tell me there was only one room, because it would be a giant waste of the forced proximity trope if there wasn't. I mean, what author would force a couple who are obviously attracted to each other together if there's going to be more than one room? And there also better have only been one bed or I want a refund."

"My life isn't a romance novel."

"Oh, really?" She crosses her arms in front of her chest. "You're technically an innkeeper. Correct?"

"Yes."

"And he's trying to buy said inn from you, a place where the entire town comes to celebrate Christmas. Is he not?"

"So?"

"You swore he was your arch nemesis until he gave you a peek behind his hard exterior last week during dance lessons. Right?"

I shrug, not giving her a response.

"This is totally the grump who saved Christmas

trope! It only follows that there was some only-one-bed action that led to incredibly hot sex. Am I right?"

I bite my lower lip, goosebumps prickling my skin at the reminder of Callum moving on top of me. Below me. Behind me. All the pleasure I experienced from his masterful touch.

When we got back here this afternoon and said our goodbyes without discussing anything further, I told myself it was probably best if I kept it quiet. Forget last night happened.

But I'm desperate to tell someone, if for no other reason than to relive one of the best nights of my life.

"The man made me see stars."

She shrieks excitedly. "It's about damn time!"

"Haley," I warn through gritted teeth, glancing around to see quite a few inquisitive eyes looking our way. No doubt the headline in tomorrow morning's newspaper will read something to the effect that a local innkeeper was found unresponsive due to multiple orgasms from a wealthy out-of-towner.

It wouldn't be that far from the truth.

"You need to keep sleeping with him," she says, not caring who might overhear. "One of us should be having good sex. Since I come with more baggage than most men want, it may as well be you."

"I don't know…"

"You enjoyed yourself, right?"

"I more than enjoyed myself." I fight to reel in my

grin, my cheeks heating as a rush of exhilaration runs through me. "The things he made me feel…" I lean closer. "I had no idea sex could be so…amazing. With Callum, it's not a question of if he can make me come but how many times."

"How many times are we talking?"

"I lost count, Haley. Between last night and this morning, not to mention a few times on the drive home, it had to be at least a nine."

"Nine?" she exclaims so loud people could probably hear her all the way in Reno. "That's not something you walk away from."

"But—"

She holds up a hand, cutting me off.

"Stop over-analyzing things. Live in the moment. Not five days from now. Hell, not even five hours from now. Just enjoy the getting while the getting's good. And based on the satisfied smile on your face, the getting's good."

"So damn good," I admit before I can stop myself.

"And based on the way that man is currently eye-fucking you from the veranda, the getting is just as good for him."

"What are you talking about?" I whirl around, my stomach fluttering when my gaze lands on Callum as he leans against the railing, a bright red scarf adding a pop of color to his charcoal coat and dark jeans.

And the look he's currently giving me makes me

think he's on the brink of ripping every inch of fabric off my body.

It's the first time I've seen him since we got back here this afternoon. I half-expected he'd pack up now that he knows I have no intention of accepting his offer until after Christmas at the earliest.

Yet, he's still here. It could just be to continue buttering up to me.

I'd like to think there's another reason he's still here.

That he couldn't stand the idea of leaving yet.

"Go get 'em, tiger," Haley encourages, gently pushing me in Callum's direction.

Despite knowing nothing good could come of this, I can't seem to do anything but walk toward him, drawn to him in ways I doubt I'll ever be able to explain.

And for the first time in my life, I'm okay with that.

"Mr. Reed," I say as I approach.

"Ms. Holley." His voice is cool. Calm. Collected.

"Are you enjoying your evening?" I ask with a cordial smile that hints at being flirtatious. "I'll admit. I'm quite surprised to see you out and about enjoying the market."

"I was admiring the view."

A shiver trickles down my spine as he rakes his appreciative gaze over me.

"And how do you find the view?"

"Absolutely stunning." He licks his lips, reminding me just how talented that tongue is. "Although, I'd like to discuss my accommodations."

"What about them?"

A sly smirk crawls across his lips. "Truthfully, after last night, I find them somewhat…lacking."

"Is that right?"

He slowly nods, his smile becoming even more devious.

"How so?"

A contemplative look crosses his face. "It's hard for me to put my finger on what exactly."

"Then perhaps I should come see for myself?" I offer demurely. "After all, it's our goal here at Holley Ridge to ensure all guests have everything they need. That any and all concerns are addressed immediately. So please allow me to address your concerns personally, Mr. Reed."

"I appreciate that, Ms. Holley."

"It's my pleasure," I purr, my pulse kicking up the longer I'm in his presence. "Shall we?" I raise an expectant brow.

He responds with a slight nod and extends his arm, allowing me to walk in front of him.

As we silently weave our way through the crowd, the air crackles with electricity, a live wire ready to snap at any second.

By the time we reach the cottage, we're both on edge, as evidenced by Callum's frantic fingers fumbling with the keycard. It feels like it takes forever for him to pull it out of his wallet. Once he does, he quickly opens the door, allowing me to enter first.

The second the door clicks closed, I face him and remove my coat, draping it on a nearby chair.

"Now, Mr. Reed," I begin, sauntering toward him. "Tell me how I can be of service to you."

He eats up the last remaining space between us, gripping my face and burrowing his fingers into my hair. "Give me this mouth."

"Yes, sir," I manage to say before he slams his lips against mine.

TWENTY

Callum

"This might be a first," Parker exhales, struggling to catch her breath as she lies in my arms, the sheets a tangled mess beneath us.

"A first?" I brush my lips against her temple, the gentleness of my touch at complete odds with the way I just fucked her.

The second I had her alone, I was a man on a mission.

I had to be, since she told me she couldn't be gone long.

But I promised I'd make her come at least twice.

I'm proud to say I more than delivered.

I've always been a bit of an overachiever. Feeling

Parker come undone three times in the span of fifteen minutes may be my proudest accomplishment to date.

"If my calculations are correct, and I'm fairly certain they are, that was the twelfth orgasm I've given you." I give her a cocky smile.

"I'm not talking about a first orgasm." She playfully swats me. "This is the first time I've had sex in one of the rooms here. And with a guest."

"You naughty minx, you." I push her onto her back and pin her beneath me. "I'm quite pleased with the deluxe package. The management team truly goes above and beyond to ensure all of my needs have been satisfied." I move my hips in languid circles, the friction causing my erection to stir once more. "In every way possible."

I curve toward her, my lips moving slowly against hers, coaxing them apart. She moans, her body melting into mine yet again. I've never been with anyone who responded this way to a mere kiss.

Which is why I shouldn't keep seeing her. Hell, I should have left once we got back from Lyden Springs. She made it quite clear she has no plans to consider my offer until after Christmas. I could use this time to go to LA, try to secure another piece of property I have my eye on down there for a new subdivision.

But I couldn't stomach the idea of leaving her. I told myself that just because she didn't want to entertain offers right now doesn't mean I should leave. If anything, I need to stay so when the time comes, she accepts my offer.

In reality, my decision had nothing to do with our professional relationship, and everything to do with what she makes me feel when I'm with her.

"What are we doing, Callum?" Parker murmurs once I bring our kiss to an end.

I don't immediately answer, searching her conflicted blue eyes.

"I don't know," I finally say with all the honesty I can muster. "But I do know I don't want to stop doing this. Not yet anyway."

"Me, neither," she confesses.

I lean my forearm on the bed beside her, smoothing a few tendrils of hair behind her ear. "So why don't we keep doing this? Enjoy the moment. Not worry about the future."

"Do you think you can do that?" She pinches her lips into a playful smirk. "You don't seem the spontaneous type. You scheduled your first kiss, for crying out loud."

"I'd proffer I was quite spontaneous last night. And just now." I gently thrust against her, causing a moan to slip from her throat.

Which has the unfortunate effect of making my erection harden even more.

That's the power this woman has over me. I feel

like a teenager going through puberty, desperate to hump anything and everything.

But in my case, I'm just desperate to hump Parker any and every chance I get.

"From the sound of things, you quite enjoy my spontaneity." I drag my tongue along her throat, relishing in the taste of her delicious skin. "Don't you?"

She cranes her head, giving me better access as she writhes beneath me. "I can't argue with that."

I nibble on the place where her neck meets her earlobe, knowing how sensitive that spot is. How much she loves when I trace circles there with my tongue.

"Then I say we keep enjoying this for the duration of my reservation. No need to place unrealistic expectations on each other. No need to make promises we'll never be able to keep. Let's just enjoy this right here. Right now. Nothing more. Okay?"

This isn't the first time I've made this kind of agreement with another woman. In my experience, I've learned it's best to set boundaries in the beginning. That way, there are no broken hearts or hurt feelings when it ends. And it always ends. I refuse to make a promise I can't keep.

I know how it feels to be on the receiving end of a broken promise.

But proposing this kind of arrangement with Parker leaves a sour taste in mouth.

What choice do I have? She deserves to be with someone whose world revolves around her. Who can give her everything she wants. Home. Love.

Family.

I can't give her that.

She parts her lips, and I brace myself for her to turn me down. Insist she deserves more than some sort of friends-with-benefits arrangement. If we can even be considered friends. I'm not sure what to consider her.

Instead, she threads her fingers into my hair, and I arch into her touch. There's something about her nails digging into my scalp that sets me off, desire heating my veins.

"It's like Haley told me earlier…," she begins in a husky voice oozing with desire.

"What's that?"

She waggles her brows. "I better get while the getting's good."

"So the getting's good?" I inch my lips back toward hers. But I don't kiss her, a whisper separating us, driving her wild with anticipation.

It's driving me wild, too. I'm desperate to taste her, to lose myself in her kiss.

But I love seeing the effect I have on her. Love

knowing I can bring her to the edge of oblivion with the mere promise of a kiss.

"So damn good," she exhales breathlessly.

"Good answer." I slam my lips against hers, our tongues tangling as I circle my hips against her. It doesn't matter I was buried deep inside of her mere minutes ago. I need more.

I fear I always will.

My tongue traces a slow path from her mouth and down the valley of her chest. When I take her nipple between my teeth, she shudders beneath me, scraping her nails down my spine.

"Callum...," she pleads. "I can't. I need to get back to work."

"I promise to make it worth your while." I slide my hand up the inside of her thigh. When I tease her clit, she no longer seems to care about what she should do. All that matters is what she *wants* to do.

If anyone deserves to do what they want, to hell with anything else, it's this woman.

"Okay," she whimpers, moving in perfect sync with my ministrations. "One more time."

"One more time," I repeat as I ease inside of her.

Although, I have a feeling I'll always need one more time with Parker Holley.

TWENTY-ONE

Parker

I finally understand why rewards are so effective when training a dog.

Over the past few days, whenever my cell has pinged with an incoming text, my heart leaps in the hopes it's from Callum, telling me there's something he needs to bring to my attention.

And every time, I happily drop whatever I'm doing and hurry to the cottage, knowing I'll be rewarded the instant he yanks me inside.

You'd think we were a bunch of hormone-crazed teenagers who just discovered sex with the amount of times we've gone at it. But I'm enjoying every damn second.

"Ms. Holley," Callum says as he opens the door

Saturday afternoon, his eyes raking down my body like an animal in heat. "To what do I owe this pleasant surprise?" He steps back to allow me to enter, but I remain on the front porch.

I understand why this would come as a surprise, since I typically barrel inside, not wanting to waste a second of our time together.

"Grab your coat."

"Are we going somewhere?" He leans against the doorjamb, crossing his arms in front of his chest, his biceps causing the material of his sweater to stretch. While I love Callum Reed in a suit, there's something about his casual look that has my heart racing, too.

"It's the Sycamore Falls Christmas Parade."

"And you want me to come with you?"

"I do."

"Is this still part of your plan to scare me away with an overabundance of holiday cheer? Because I have to confess…"

He pushes off the doorway and nuzzles my neck. I should resist him, considering we're out in the open. But most people have already left for the parade.

"These days, I have a renewed appreciation for the holiday season. Particularly sexy blondes wearing an elf costume."

I playfully bat my lashes, the corner of my mouth tugging upward in a suggestive grin. My fingertips trace the outline of his sweater, relishing in the warmth of his chest underneath.

"Would you like me to change into that costume, Mr. Reed? As you know, we're all about delivering an exceptional guest experience here at Holley Ridge." My voice is low. Breathy. Sensual. "It's our hope to go above and beyond. To ensure your stay here is one you'll never forget."

"Ms. Holley…" The muscles in his face tighten, his pupils dilating. "If you put on that elf costume, I can guarantee the only parade you'll be attending is a parade of orgasms."

"Perhaps later then."

"I'm going to hold you to that." He waggles his brows, grinning mischievously.

"Good. Now put on your coat and shoes."

I purposefully stay on the porch, knowing if I step inside, the chances of us making it to the Christmas parade will be drastically diminished. Once he's ready, he reappears in the doorway. But instead of stepping onto the porch, he wraps his hand around my forearm, yanking me inside.

"Callum, what are you—"

He erases my question with a light kiss, gently cradling my face. I surrender to him with a contented sigh, wrapping an arm around his shoulder and drawing him closer. He tastes of mint, coffee, and something that's uniquely Callum Reed.

Even though we're already running late, I allow myself this brief moment, knowing in less than a week he'll check out and go on with his life, forgetting about the time he spent here.

But me? I doubt I'll ever forget the Christmas the grump stole my heart.

"I couldn't go all day without kissing you," he explains as he rests his forehead on mine, pausing to catch his breath. "Figured I'd steal one to hold me over, although now it only makes me want more." He tenderly traces a line down my jaw, the affection in his gaze almost too much. "I'll always want more of you, Parker."

He touches his lips back to mine, his kiss slow and measured, before reluctantly pulling away. "Shall we?"

I briefly contemplate blowing off the parade. After all, it's the perfect opportunity to be able to enjoy each other for an extended period of time, since everyone will be downtown for the next few hours.

But I want Callum to experience the excitement and community of the Sycamore Falls Christmas Parade. I always looked forward to it when I was a little girl. I still do, even as an adult. I want to share this with him.

Our steps are slow as we meander through my practically abandoned property underneath the ceiling of a picturesque blue sky. Any other Saturday afternoon, it would be swarming with people enjoying the Christmas market, trying their hand at ice skating, making holiday-inspired crafts, or waiting to meet Santa.

But I close down so everyone can enjoy the parade.

"It's so…quiet," Callum remarks. "Peaceful. It must look amazing in the fall."

"You have no idea. All the oranges, yellows, and reds. It's probably my favorite time of year."

"Not Christmas?" he teases, nudging me.

"No," I draw out as we walk past the inn and down the path toward Main Street. "I do love Christmas, too. But I'll always have a soft spot for those first few weeks of fall. When the weather cools down and you can pull on a big sweater and fuzzy socks. And that first fire of the season." I briefly close my eyes, almost able to smell leaves burning in the air.

A part of me wishes I could show him how beautiful this place is in the fall. Could snuggle up next to him after a long day of work in front of a roaring fire. Could fall asleep in his arms as he keeps me warm.

Suddenly, a pair of lips cover mine, and I stiffen, inhaling a sharp breath.

"Sorry." Callum pulls back. "You just… You looked so damn gorgeous that I forgot where we were for a second. Forgot where *I* was."

"It's okay. You can kiss me. You don't have to, of

course," I add quickly. "I just want to keep any overt displays of affection under wraps at Holley Ridge."

"Isn't that where we are?"

"Technically, this is the property of the Town of Sycamore Falls."

"So we're not on Holley Ridge?"

I slowly shake my head. "We're not on Holley Ridge."

Callum doesn't waste any time in enveloping me in his embrace and crushing his lips back to mine. As much as I hate the barrier of our heavy coats between us, there's something intoxicating about kissing Callum out in the open. It makes me wish I could do it more.

But we agreed. No expectations. No promises for a future.

"Come on," I say, fighting to free myself from him. "The parade's about to start." I grab his hand, tugging him toward downtown. The sound of excited voices and Christmas music gets louder the closer we get. "You don't want to miss the skateboarding pugs."

"Skateboarding…pugs?"

"They're a Sycamore Falls tradition. Mr. Jensen saw a pair of surfing pugs on television a few years ago and decided to train his dogs to skateboard. They're rather good."

"I have a feeling this is going to be quite the experience," he remarks with a heartwarming smile. It's so different from the cold, heartless man I thought he was.

A few weeks ago, if someone told me I'd be walking down Main Street holding Callum's hand as we waited for the Christmas Parade to start, I would have nearly died with laughter. Then I would have asked for some of whatever they'd taken to cause such an improbable hallucination.

But there's no one else I want to be with right now.

There's no one else I can picture doing this with.

Which is only going to make it harder to say goodbye when he leaves in a few short days.

TWENTY-TWO

Callum

I haven't spent much time in downtown Sycamore Falls since arriving here over a week ago. Sure, I'd done my research on the area before making an offer on Holley Ridge. I knew it was a historic downtown area with all the amenities one would expect in a small town. Diner. Coffee shop. Bookstore. Hardware store. Even a brewery.

But walking along the sidewalks with Parker on my arm is a completely different experience.

There's something magical about this place. It's like I've stepped back into a simpler time. A slower time. There are no disagreements about politics. No discussions about the latest headlines. Everyone here seems to genuinely like each other.

And they all adore Parker.

I don't blame them.

I kind of do, too.

"Are you ready to bolt?" Parker asks as we sneak through the crowd.

By the sheer number of people swarming downtown, I'd guess the entire population of Sycamore Falls is here. Probably even quite a few people from neighboring communities, too.

"What makes you say that?"

"Figured all the Christmas cheer might be too much for your Grinchy tendencies."

"If it means spending time with you, I'm willing to suffer."

I'd happily endure much worse than large crowds and an overabundance of Christmas spirit if it's with Parker at my side.

"This is us here." She guides me down an alley between two brick storefronts, stopping in front of a metal door and opening it.

I follow her up several narrow flights of stairs before emerging onto a rooftop bar, heaters warming the space that's decorated for the season, twinkling lights strung overhead with garland lining the tables.

"This is the Wicked Hop, a local brewery my friend owns," she explains, steering me toward a large gathering of people. A few high-top tables are set up in the center, along with a long table off to the side, boasting a wide assortment of *hors d'oeuvres*.

"Auntie Parker! Auntie Parker!" a little girl says excitedly as we approach, all eyes turning our way.

Parker crouches down, her expression bright as she holds out her arms for the small redhead, who I recognize as Haley's daughter.

"Hiya, Magpie." She nuzzles her nose. "Are you excited about the parade?"

"Yes!"

"What are you most excited about?"

The little girl scrunches her brow, as if the answer could mean life or death. Finally, she announces, "Santa. But Mr. Jensen's pugs are a close second."

Parker laughs, the sound carrying through the air. I can't help but admire her. She looks so carefree. So happy. What I wouldn't give to freeze this moment, live in it for as long as possible, if for no other reason than to relish in her joy. The smooth curve of her cheeks. The sparkle in her eyes. The way her lips curl tightly in the corners.

"Maggie, this is my good friend, Callum."

The little girl looks my way, scrutinizing me with an intensity I don't quite expect from a small child. Then again, in my experience, kids are much more honest and perceptive than adults.

"But you're not green."

I glance at Parker, brows furrowed. "Am I supposed to be?"

"Mommy says you're the Grinch and you're trying to steal Christmas from Auntie Parker."

I part my lips to explain, but before I can, Parker intervenes. "He's not trying to steal Christmas. He just thinks Holley Ridge is so pretty that more people might want to be able to visit." Parker glances my way, treating me to a smile that nearly turns my insides to mush. "Isn't that right?"

"She's right," I say, although I feel worse than the Grinch when he told Cindy Lou he was taking her tree up to the North Pole to fix a light.

Maggie toils this over in her head for a moment, then nods, focusing her attention back on Parker. "Can I come ice skate after the parade?"

She carefully lowers her back to her feet. "You'll have to ask your mama."

"Okay." Spinning, she runs off into the crowd of people, all of them doting on her.

"Thanks for that," I say in a low voice.

"For what?"

"Not making me out to be an asshole."

"Like the Grinch, you're just misunderstood. Plus, over the past few days, I've seen that heart of yours grow a few sizes." She pats my chest. "Come on. I want you to meet everyone."

As she loops her arm through mine and introduces me to her friends, a hollow ache forms in the pit of my stomach. I almost wish she would make me out to be an asshole. It might make the knowledge that I'll soon be leaving here a little easier to swallow.

A few people give me a look of reproach, especially Beckham, who I learn is the head winemaker at the vineyard that produces the bottle we shared the other night at dinner. It's obvious he doesn't agree with what I'm doing.

I'm starting to question it myself.

I've been doing this for the better part of the past decade. Not once have I ever raised a single doubt about finding a property on the brink of foreclosure and making the owners an offer to sell before it goes to auction. It's always been a numbers game to me.

And numbers don't lie.

It's why I like them.

There's no uncertainty. No ambiguity. No obscurity. It's clear. Evident. Predictable.

Lately, my life has been anything but predictable. All because of Parker Holley.

Now, every time one of my employees sends me a report on a potential new acquisition, I don't just see the numbers. I see Parker. See her staff. See the memories she's made.

"I understand my daughter called you the Grinch," Haley says, sidling up to me a while later as I lean against the rooftop railing, taking in the sights of the Christmas parade below me.

I look away from the Sycamore Falls High School Marching Band as they entertain the crowd with a rendition of "Santa Claus is Coming to Town".

"She didn't say anything that's not true."

"Actually..." Haley chews on her lower lip. "You're not as big of a Grinch as I originally thought. I misjudged you, and I'm sorry. She heard that from me. When you have kids, you'll learn nothing you say is safe around them. They will repeat everything. And usually at the absolute worst time."

"I'll take that under advisement." I chuckle, about to return my attention to the parade when laughter erupts from a few feet away.

I glance toward the bar, not surprised to see that Parker got held up talking to a few locals. I've gotten used to that today. Everyone wants to talk to her. Wants to be near her.

I can't blame them.

I do, too.

"People love her," I remark as she catches my gaze, sending a smile my way before resuming her conversation with another one of the Lawrence siblings. Hayden, I think she said his name was.

"They do," Haley agrees. "Parker Holley is highly admired and respected here in town. Even before she took out that mortgage so she could keep paying all her employees when the world shut down."

I inhale a sharp breath and dart my wide eyes to hers. "What are you talking about?"

Haley looks at me incredulously, as if I'm asking about the color of the sky or who the jolly man in the red suit is.

"The mortgage she owes. You do know what she owes on the property. Otherwise, you wouldn't be trying to buy it from her."

"I know. I just…" I step closer, lowering my voice. "She used it to cover payroll for her employees during the pandemic? I thought…" I look away, the weight of this truth settling on my chest.

I've heard countless stories about people losing their businesses over the past few years. Hell, I've *bene-fited* from hundreds of people losing their businesses.

But the idea of Parker also losing everything she worked for, all because she selflessly took out a loan to provide for her employees, guts me.

"I thought that was to pay for the construction on the inn," I say finally, shifting my eyes back to Haley.

"The first one was."

"So the money she owes to the bank is…"

"Because she made sure her employees were able to put food on the table and keep a roof over their heads."

"I didn't know," I exhale.

"Now you do. We've all tried to pitch in where we can. Of course, she's refused all donations, insisting if people want to help, they can come to Holley Ridge or spread the word. If anyone deserves a miracle right now, it's her."

I slowly nod, overwhelmed by the magnitude of Parker's heart. I shouldn't be surprised. Based on what I've learned about her in the short time I've known her, she tends to put everyone else first. Will bend over backward to help anyone who needs it.

But knowing how much she sacrificed for her employees makes me want to do something to help her.

Haley's right.

If anyone deserves a miracle, it's Parker.

And maybe there's something I can do to help with that miracle.

Even if it means she'll no longer need to sell to me.

TWENTY-THREE

Parker

"Parker," Callum calls out as I walk through Holley Ridge Monday afternoon. A grin tugs on my lips from the mere sound of his voice.

The past few days have felt like something out of a Hallmark movie. Or even a book.

Not one of Grandma Estelle's monster romance books, though.

A heartwarming romance that's made me swoon more times than I can count.

Given me more orgasms than I can count, too.

Callum and I have spent every possible moment together. Snuggling close as we watched the Christmas parade. Holding hands as we walked down Main Street. Stealing a kiss in the corner of the hardware store as he told me stories from his house-flipping days.

The more I learn about him, the more I'm beginning to dread Thursday.

But we agreed.

This ends when his reservation does.

Although a part of me would love to extend his stay here indefinitely, regardless of how unlikely that is.

"Mr. Reed," I greet him, resisting the urge to throw my arms around him and lose myself in his kiss. I've been craving another one since I slipped out of his bed before the sun rose this morning.

"This is Eloise Moore." Callum gestures to the petite blonde at his side who appears to be about my age. "She has a wildly popular YouTube channel where she explores hidden gems all around the world in the hopes of encouraging people to step off the beaten path, so to speak. Eloise, this is Parker Holley."

I give Callum a curious stare before I extend my hand toward her. "It's a pleasure to meet you."

"You, too," she responds as we shake. "Callum told me all about this place and was quite adamant I needed to see it, especially this time of year."

She tears her gaze from me to take in the festive atmosphere. Colorful holiday ornaments and other crafts cover the tables lining the market, the smell of freshly made doughnuts wafting through the air.

"He was right. It's amazing." She returns her attention to me. "How long has this been going on?"

I steal another confused glance at Callum, but his wide smile gives nothing away.

"Even before she was born," he answers when I remain bewildered. "It was once a horse boarding facility. Her parents always decorated extensively for the holidays. Over the years, they started opening it up for visitors to come look at the lights, eventually adding a market, ice skating rink, and other activities."

"It's fabulous. Exactly the kind of thing my viewers love. When did you open the inn?"

"About five years ago," I answer, finally able to overcome my shock and confusion enough to respond. "I restored the barn first. My mother always dreamed of hosting weddings here. Thought the lake with the mountains in the distance would make a beautiful backdrop."

"It's stunning," Eloise remarks.

"Unfortunately, there aren't a lot of hotels around here, so it wasn't too convenient for those coming from out of town. After a year, I began construction on the inn." I gesture behind us to the main building. "It started with just twenty rooms, but as need increased, I added two additional wings, each with ten rooms." My expression falls. "That was around the same time the world shut down. Both the tourism and wedding industries were hit particularly hard. Just my luck, those are my two sources of income."

Eloise offers me a sympathetic look. "Callum mentioned you took out an additional mortgage in order to pay your employees during the shutdown."

I snap my head toward him, eyes wide, mouth agape.

How did he know? I never told him about that. Sure, I shared that I'd used my inheritance to restore the barn, then took out a mortgage to build the inn. Those were smart business decisions, ones that would allow me to recoup the expenses in order to pay back the loans.

This mortgage wasn't.

"I did," I admit. "We may have been forced to shut down, but I couldn't let my staff struggle. They have families to provide for."

"That's remarkable."

"That's Parker," Callum interjects, placing his hand on the small of my back. "She's quite remark-able. And caring. Always giving back to the commu-nity. Every year, she holds a carnival for foster kids. Even goes out of her way to make sure at least one gift off their wish list is waiting underneath the tree Christmas morning." Affection swirls in his dark eyes. "She's unlike anyone I've ever met."

Warmth spreads through my chest, my heart swelling with emotion.

I wish it didn't. Wish his words of praise didn't hit me any differently than when anyone else says something similar about everything I do to give back to this community.

"After all you've given others, I'd love to be able to help give back to you," Eloise says, pulling my attention back to her.

"I'm not looking for a handout or for people to view me as a charity case. Like I tell everyone, if you want to help, just come to Holley Ridge. Have dinner. Go ice skating. Get something in exchange for your hard-earned dollars."

"Callum told me that. Which is why I'm here. To help spread the word." She holds up a DSLR camera on a handheld tripod. "Do you mind if I do some exploring? My viewers will love a place like this. They're always looking for ways to celebrate the season, and this is perfect."

"Of course. Thank you. Truly." I shift my gaze to Callum. "You have no idea what this means to me."

"No. Thank you." She looks into the distance, drawing in a slow breath. "These days, Christmas spirit is hard to come by. This place reminds me of what it was like being a kid during this time of year."

"I hope you enjoy yourself. If you need anything and can't find me, you can ask any of my staff members. They know how to reach me."

"Will do."

I watch as she takes off toward the Christmas market, a renewed hope filling me that maybe it will all work out in the end. That maybe this is the miracle I've been praying for.

Facing Callum, I tilt my head back, meeting his eyes. "Why are you doing this?"

"Because you deserve a miracle, Parker." He runs his hands down my arms. "After Haley told me about—"

"Of course," I exhale.

I should have known Haley would let the truth slip. It's not like I specifically told her not to tell him how I ended up in over my head in debt. I just never thought it would come up. Didn't think he'd hang around long enough to learn. Didn't think he cared enough, either.

It's obvious he does care.

Quite a bit.

"I'm sorry. I just…" He tightens his hold on me and peers at me with an emotion I can't quite label. An emotion I don't *want* to label. "I couldn't stand by and not do something, especially when Haley told me how you've refused donations."

"There are people out there starving and living on the streets. They need it more than I do."

"Which is why I wanted to do this for you. If you won't accept my money, you can accept my connections. Eloise owes me. She used to be one of my tenants and constantly needed me to unclog her shower drain." He playfully rolls his eyes. "Now I'm glad I helped her so she could return the favor. For you."

I swallow hard through the tightness in my throat. I have to work hard not to let the tears pooling in my eyes spill over. This is the absolute last thing I expected Callum to do for me, considering his reason for being here in the first place.

"Shouldn't you be doing something to convince me to sell? Not do something that might make it so I don't have to?"

"What fun is it if you don't even have a fighting chance?" With a smile, he drops his hold on me, continuing along the path toward the restored barn. I scramble to catch up, still trying to wrap my head around this. Trying to figure out what game he's playing.

Or maybe he isn't.

Maybe this is just the type of person he is.

"Is that the only reason you're doing this?" I joke, playfully nudging him. "To give me a fighting chance so it feels better when I come up short and finally agree to sell?"

He stops walking, pulling me along with him. The intensity in his stare causes my heart to race, every cell in my body vibrating with an unexpected charge.

When he reaches for my face, I don't back away,

despite being out in the open. He's leaving in a few days. Who cares if guests see him holding me?

"Actually, the idea of you coming up short feels awful," he admits, his voice heavy with sincerity.

"Even though you'd make millions if I did?"

"What can I say?" He moves his hands to my hips. "You've made me realize there are more important things than working all the time. You'd think I would have learned that lesson after—"

"Hey." I rest my hand on his chest, and my eyes lock with his. "That wasn't your fault. Do you work too much? Maybe. I'm guilty of the same thing. Hell, the other night was the first night I spent away from here since I started running this place."

"But it was a business meeting," he taunts.

I adjust my stance, dragging my body closer to his. "I don't know how you run your business meetings, but I typically don't end up naked in bed at the end of it."

"I didn't hear you complaining." He inches closer, his lips skimming my neck. "In fact, I was wondering if you had some time to spare right now. I do think there's more to discuss."

I purse my lips. "Like what?"

"Like updating your property management software."

"I love when you talk hospitality to me," I reply

breathlessly, and a deep chuckle tumbles from his throat.

"Adding a few in-room amenities, such as mini bars, which will allow you to increase your average room rate."

"God yes." I flutter my eyelids, all but moaning the words, feigning to be in the throes of ecstasy. "Now you're talking."

His Adam's apple bobs in a hard swallow, his jaw tightening as he leans closer still, the warmth of his breath hitting my lips, making me salivate for his kiss.

"Working with similar properties to offer some sort of loyalty scheme."

"Fuck yes," I whimper. "That's sounds incredible."

"Goddamn, Parker," he growls, looping his arm around my waist and yanking my body flush with his, his need for me pressing into my stomach.

I've never been with someone who was so unashamed in displaying his desire for me. Who has no problem telling me how much he craves me. Who looks at me in a way that makes me think I'm the only person in his entire universe who matters.

"You drive me crazy. You know that, right?"

"I *feel* that," I tease with a flirtatious waggle of my brow. "It *is* quite hard to miss. And quite hard."

He throws his head back, his laughter echoing in

the winter air. Being with Callum is just so effortless. So easy.

"So… About that meeting?" he prods once his laughter dies down, a single brow arched.

I drape an arm over his shoulder and hoist myself onto my toes. "I believe I can squeeze you in, Mr. Reed."

TWENTY-FOUR

Parker

I lean against the edge of the ice skating rink, taking in the sights and sounds of Holley Ridge. The area bustles with activity — families bundled up in their winter coats, couples holding hands, kids running around. I marvel at the sheer number of people here, even on a Wednesday afternoon. It's busier than I've ever seen it, even during the days leading up to Christmas or our annual Trick-or-Treat event.

Admittedly, I didn't get my hopes up after Eloise Moore paid my quirky little ranch a visit.

But all it took was a few videos encouraging people to come to Holley Ridge this Christmas season to make a difference.

Overnight, crowds started to swell until we had no choice but to create a line at the gate just to keep the numbers manageable.

As great as it's been for business, I don't know if it will be enough. Not with the amount I owe to the bank.

Which is why I spent the majority of the morning reviewing Callum's offer. My lawyer insists it's more than generous and would allow me to pay off all my debts, as well as leave me with a substantial amount of savings to live on while I figure out what's next.

I just don't know if I can give up.

Don't know if I can let go of this place.

"Have you made a decision?"

At the sound of Estelle's voice, I tear my gaze away from Callum leading Maggie around the ice with extreme patience and care. I was surprised he even knew how to skate, let alone learn he'd played hockey from childhood through college.

He's definitely not who I thought he was.

"I'm still torn," I admit with a long sigh. "Based on what we've taken in the past few days, it will still take a miracle to come up with what I need. I could call the bank, see if they're willing to work with me a little longer, but—"

"I'm not talking about the offer." She narrows her gaze on me. "I'm talking about that tall drink of water you've been shtupping every chance you've gotten this week." She nods in Callum's general direction.

"Shtupping?"

"Would you prefer I call it something else? Checking the oil? Doing the no-pants dance? Hiding the bishop? Wetting the willy? Or do you just prefer to call it what it really is? Some good ol' fashioned fucking."

"Grandma Estelle!"

I can't pretend to be offended or surprised. I've grown to appreciate her somewhat eccentric mannerisms.

Including her knowledge of far too many colorful phrases for sex.

She places her glove-covered hand over mine. "I'm happy for you, Parker."

"We both are," Haley adds, joining us and handing me a coffee.

"It's not like that," I remind them, bringing the paper cup to my mouth, savoring in the warm liquid.

"Oh, no?" Grandma Estelle tilts her head, giving me a skeptical look. "Then tell me what it *is* like. From what I've observed of the two of you, you're both quite smitten."

"It's just a fling while he's in town. Once he checks out, it's over. We agreed. It's too complicated otherwise."

"Why? Because he's trying to buy this place? If

you ask me, that's the universe giving you the solution you were looking for."

"What are you talking about?" I furrow my brow, glancing at Haley.

"You asked the universe for a solution to your problem," Grandma Estelle responds. "Did you not?"

"You know I did."

"And the universe presented you with a solution to your problem." Haley shifts her gaze in Callum's direction.

I follow her line of sight, my insides warming when he beams a charismatic smile that would have me dropping my panties if we were alone.

"You think some real estate development firm wanting to swoop in and buy this property is the solution I need?"

"I do," Haley says evenly.

"We both do," Grandma Estelle adds.

I blink, unable to believe what I'm hearing. If anyone was going to fight alongside me until the bitter end, I would have expected it to be Estelle. She was my mother's best friend. Helped my parents transform this property. I pictured her strapping herself to the giant Norway spruce as an act of protest when the bulldozers showed up.

Now she's telling me Callum's offer is the universe giving me what I need?

"How? I don't—"

"Your mother often said the universe works in mysterious ways.," Grandma Estelle explains. "That sometimes we think we need one thing when in reality what we really need is something else. I think this is the universe showing you what's important. And it's not a piece of property."

"But it's not just a piece of property," I protest. "My parents built this into what it is today. This was their dream." I gesture at all the people roaming the grounds. "This was my childhood. All the memories…" I shake my head, struggling to come to terms with the idea of it all going away, even if it's becoming more of a reality every day.

"And you'll always have those," Grandma Estelle insists.

"No one can take them away," Haley adds.

"Maybe this is the universe's way of telling you that you've been clinging to those memories for too long now." Grandma Estelle touches her hand to my arm. "That you've been clinging to the past for too long now. Maybe it's time to stop living in the past. To start looking toward the future. Start making memories of your own instead of doing everything you can to keep your parents' memory alive."

"I don't—"

"Your mother dreamed of restoring the barn in the hopes of hosting weddings here," Grandma Estelle interrupts. "Isn't that right?"

I give a subtle nod.

"She hoped to see you get married here, Parker. She would hate to know you've sacrificed your own happiness just so you could ensure your parents' dreams for this property are realized. You were always the most important thing to them. They would have given up everything to make sure you were happy." Grandma Estelle waves her hand at my surroundings. "Including all of this. The sleigh rides. The tree. The pictures with Santa. It's all great. But it's not what's important."

I part my lips, about to renew my argument. I can't, though. She's right. Hell, if my parents were still alive, I have no doubt they'd tell me the same thing.

"Even so, that doesn't change things with Callum." I straighten my spine, smoothing a hand down my coat. "We had an understanding when we started...whatever this is. We agreed it would end when he checked out."

"But you made that agreement almost a week ago," Haley reminds me. "Things may have changed. I know they've changed for you."

I shrug, pretending to remain unaffected, not wanting to admit that, over the past several days, Callum Reed has weaseled his way into my heart. Every conversation, every smile, every thoughtful word has made me care about him more. Even without him going out of his way to ask Eloise Moore to help, I would have felt this way. But knowing he was willing to risk his own future plans for this property ripped through the last remnants of the wall surrounding my heart.

"Maybe they've changed for him, too," Haley continues. "You'll never know unless you ask. Do you really want him to leave and always wonder what if?"

I slowly turn my eyes back toward the rink, my throat tightening at the idea of saying goodbye to Callum tomorrow morning and never experiencing anything remotely close to what I do with him.

But can I really put my heart on the line, knowing he has the power to destroy it?

Can I really risk it all with him?

TWENTY-FIVE

Parker

I shouldn't be this nervous. It's only dinner with the guy I've been sleeping with the past week.

But it doesn't matter how many times I tell myself it's only dinner.

Deep down, I know it's so much more than that. Especially with Grandma Estelle's and Haley's words weighing heavy on my mind. Can I really take that leap, share my true feelings in the hopes Callum has also had a change of heart?

Throughout the day, I've tried to convince myself there's no way Callum Reed is the solution to my problem. He's trying to buy this place from me, for crying out loud.

Then again, he hasn't done anything lately to

indicate he's still trying to buy Holley Ridge. If anything, his actions have demonstrated he wants me to hold on to it.

But is that what I want?

I'm no longer sure.

A gentle tapping on the door brings me out of my thoughts, and my pulse immediately kicks up. On a long exhale, I run my hands down my dress, checking my reflection one last time. I almost didn't get dressed up tonight. That would make this a real date. I've refused to label anything as a date. We may fuck, but a date means feelings.

I'm not supposed to have any feelings for Callum.

But when I open the door and see him standing outside my apartment looking more handsome than I thought possible with his dark suit and festive tie, holding a stunning bouquet of flowers, it's a losing battle.

I've already fallen hard, despite resisting it at every turn.

"Wow," Callum exhales, his eyes tracing over the little black dress that accentuates my curves. "You look…" He licks his lips as he brings his gaze back to mine. Then he leans in to brush a soft kiss against my cheek. "You're stunning, Parker."

I squeeze my eyes shut, pushing down the wave of emotions threatening to overwhelm me at the reminder that this is one of the last times I'll ever hear him call me beautiful.

A voice in my head that sounds eerily like Grandma Estelle reminds me it doesn't have to be.

But I silence it as he clears his throat and hands me the bouquet of red roses. "These are for you."

"Thank you." I turn and grab a vase from the kitchen, setting the flowers in water. "Ready?"

"Always."

He helps me into my coat and we head to the lobby. But instead of walking toward the parking lot, he steers me out onto the veranda.

"I thought we were having dinner."

"We are."

"But—"

"While I'm sure the restaurants in town are quite good, if this is to be my last opportunity to have dinner with you, I'm not taking you somewhere you eat all the time. You deserve to be spoiled. So that's what I plan to do tonight."

A part of me wishes he'd just take me to one of the casual restaurants in town. It would make our inevitable separation much easier to swallow.

We walk in comfortable silence along the dirt path toward the cottage. It's bittersweet to think that, starting tomorrow, I won't be able to knock on the door and have Callum yank me inside for a quickie before I go back to work.

It's not just the sex I'll miss.

It's the passion.

I've never experienced such hunger and intensity before.

But is it enough?

As I step inside the cottage, my eyes adjust to the dim lighting. A fire flickers in the gas fireplace, the dining room table already set with a few candles. The distinct notes of jazz-inspired Christmas songs fill the air, everything about it oozing romance.

God, I wish it didn't.

It's only going to make me want more of this.

"Let me take your coat," Callum offers, and I allow him to help me before he shrugs out of his own. "Wine?"

"I'd love some."

He slips into the kitchen and makes quick work of the cork on a bottle of red wine I recognize as being the same one we ordered during that first dinner. After pouring some into two glasses, he hands me one.

"To our last night together. Thanks for making my stay here so memorable."

I clink my glass with his before taking a slow sip of my wine, doing my best to mask how much I hate the idea of this being our last night together, since he doesn't seem the least bit upset about it.

I'm probably just another in a long line of women

he's met in his travels who he'll now walk away from without a single look back.

I can't fault him for it. When we started down this path, I knew the score. Knew we'd go back to our lives when it was over. I can't be mad he doesn't show any indication he's changed his mind. I'm the one who wants to rewrite the rules.

"It smells delicious," I comment in an attempt to think about something else. "You don't strike me as the type who spends much time in the kitchen."

"Haven't you learned by now?" He narrows his eyes, a seductive gleam within.

"What's that?"

He loops his free arm around me and nuzzles my neck. "I'm just full of surprises, Ms. Holley." He doesn't immediately pull back, lingering long enough to jumpstart my libido. "But you're right." He abruptly drops his hold on me. "I typically don't spend much time in the kitchen. Don't get me wrong," he adds quickly. "I'm not a horrible cook. I can make a pretty decent steak. But I want tonight to be special."

"Why?" I ask, almost hoping he'll tell me he's doing all of this because he doesn't want this to end, either. That he wants to find a way to make it work, despite all the obstacles between us.

As he rakes his gaze over my face and a hint of

that same emotion I've seen on occasion flickers in his eyes, I think he's about to do just that.

Then he pushes out a breath and shakes his head. "You spend all day putting everyone else first. It's only right I put you first tonight. Which is why I conned your chef into making us dinner."

"You did?"

"Of course." With a hand on my lower back, he leads me to the table, pulling out my chair. Once I'm situated, he heads back into the kitchen, grabbing a mitt and removing a few dishes from the oven.

He returns to the table and sets one in front of me. "The plate might be a little warm. I only had it in the oven at a low temperature so it wouldn't get cold."

"Thank you." I shift my gaze to my dish, my heart squeezing. "You had Jeffrey make lamb?"

Callum sits across from me and grabs my hand, our fingers intertwining. "I told you I wanted tonight to be special. I asked him to make something you'd like. Something you'll always remember."

"This is what my mama made on Christmas every year." I survey the dish. "It even looks like her recipe.

"It is." His lips curve in the corners. "I asked Grandma Estelle for it."

The fact that Callum went above and beyond means more than he'll ever know. I've never been with someone who actually put in this kind of effort.

Who actually seemed to care.

"Thank you," I say with a slight quiver.

"Anything for you, Parker."

TWENTY-SIX

Callum

"I can't remember the last time I've had that lamb," Parker says after practically licking her plate clean. "I tried making it after my mom passed away, but it never came out right. But Jeffrey..." She dabs at her lips, then takes another drink of her wine. "He did great."

"I'm glad you enjoyed it." I lean back as I admire her, wanting to etch a memory of this moment in my mind.

I hate that this is the last night I'll get to see that smile light up her face. As I've reminded myself time and again, she deserves more than I can give her.

"It was amazing. Everything about tonight has been amazing, Callum. Thank you."

"You're very welcome." I hold her gaze for another beat, then push to my feet.

"The night's not over yet." I glance at the clock over the mantle. "By my count, I still have ten hours until I need to catch my flight. And I have a few more surprises up my sleeve." I extend my hand toward her.

"And what would that be?" Her skin is soft as she places her hand in mine, allowing me to help her up.

"You'll find out soon." I move toward the closet and grab our coats.

"Are we going somewhere?" She steps toward me, and I help her into her coat.

"Just outside."

"Like, to the Christmas market?"

Chuckling under my breath, I put on my own coat. "Certainly not. While my time here has made me appreciate the season…" I cup her cheek, urging her lips closer. "I have no plans to share you with anyone else tonight. For the next several hours, you're mine."

"Yours," she whimpers as I cover her mouth in a brief kiss.

"Come on." I steer her toward the back door and open it, allowing her to walk out in front of me. I grab the basket I'd placed on the side table earlier and join her on the patio.

"A fire pit?" She lowers herself onto the wicker couch.

I sit beside her, holding up the basket. "And s'mores. Someone once told me you can't have a fire pit without s'mores."

"They sound incredibly intelligent," she remarks.

"Oh, she is." I rummage through the ingredients I'd packed, ripping open the bag of marshmallows. "She's quite smart. And funny. And beautiful." I lift my gaze to meet hers. "So damn beautiful."

"Callum…" Her lower lip quivers.

"But that's not why I think she's amazing," I continue, sliding a marshmallow onto a long metal rod and handing it to her. She holds it over the flame, looking between me and the fire.

"It's not?"

"No." I shake my head, little sparks of red, orange, and blue dancing in the air as I roast my marshmallow. "It's her heart." I return my eyes to hers, my throat closing up in an effort to contain whatever emotion is trying to escape. "I've never met anyone so caring. So compassionate. So warm. She had every reason to hate me. Still does. But I'm glad she doesn't."

I wish I could say more than this. Wish I could tell her we'll find a way to make it work.

But I can't.

"How do you know she doesn't?" she snips back sarcastically, cutting through the tension, much to my relief.

I chuckle as I check on my marshmallow, removing it from the fire now that it's tinted brown.

"I don't know for certain."

I set out a couple of plates with graham crackers and chocolate. Parker slides her marshmallow on top of the chocolate, covering it with another graham cracker. I do the same.

"I just hope she doesn't. I *have* given her quite a few orgasms. I think that earns me a few points."

"Maybe." She winks and takes a bite out of her s'more.

When she darts out her tongue to catch a stray bit of sticky marshmallow, every muscle in my body tenses, screaming at me to throw her onto her back and explore each inch of her beautiful body.

But I want tonight to be different.

Most of our time together has been spent having sex. Sure, there was the afternoon of the Christmas parade and the occasional run-ins on her property. For the most part, our encounters have entailed frantically ripping off each other's clothes, desperate to get our fill of each other before Parker needed to get back to her responsibilities.

That's not the case right now.

Tonight I have something I haven't had since we were snowed in together.

Her undivided attention.

And I plan on enjoying every second I can until I leave for the airport.

"You were right," I remark once we finish eating, both of us having roasted quite a few more marshmallows as we simply enjoyed each other's company.

"What's that?"

"You can't have a fire pit without s'mores. They go hand-in-hand."

"I couldn't agree more." Humor dances in her eyes. "Unless you have facial hair, I guess. You've got some stuck."

She rests her hand on my cheek as she grazes the pad of her thumb against my lower lip, wiping away a smudge of melted marshmallow.

It's a relatively innocent gesture, nothing sensual or erotic about it.

But it ignites something inside me, desire cascading through me.

I wrap my fingers around her wrist, not letting her pull her hand away. As much as I've tried to wait, spend some time with her outside of the bedroom, we only have a few hours left together. Minutes, really.

I need her skin on mine as much as possible in the little time that remains.

Moving my free hand to her hip, I yank her on top of me in one swift move, forcing her legs to straddle me. A delicious whimper falls from her throat when she feels just how much I crave her.

I peer deep into her gaze, her blue eyes holding me hostage, making me feel like she's able to see directly into my soul.

In this moment, I'm convinced she can do just that, and with more accuracy than anyone I've met before.

Even Sadie.

Which is precisely why this needs to end. Why I need to walk away now. Cut our losses before we get in too deep.

Although, with every minute that passes, I'm beginning to think I'm already in deeper than I originally intended. I haven't had feelings for a single woman since Sadie.

Didn't think it was possible.

Why this woman?

Why now?

Not wanting to think about that a moment longer, I slam my lips against hers, her tongue tangling, caressing, searching. She tastes of chocolate, sugar, and something that's pure Parker.

Something I want to bottle up and drown in when the loneliness finds me in the days and months to come.

"I was trying to wait..." I pepper kisses along her jawline, nibbling on her earlobe.

I've only known her mere weeks, yet her body is so familiar. So responsive.

As if I've known her my entire life.

As if she were made for me.

As if the universe sent her to me.

"Didn't want you to think I only like you for sex." I grip her face in both hands. "But I need to be inside you, Parker. More than I need my next damn breath."

Her lips skim mine in a light touch that still manages to send desire unfurling inside of me.

"Then have me."

TWENTY-SEVEN

Parker

Callum doesn't waste any time, jumping to his feet and pulling me with him so swiftly I barely manage to keep up as we stumble back inside the cottage. We hurriedly rid ourselves of our shoes and coats, tossing them into a pile on the floor before he crashes his lips against mine.

He moves his hands to my ass and hoists me up, forcing my legs around his waist. With quick steps, he carries me into the bedroom, his mouth not leaving mine until he lowers me to my feet to shrug off his suit jacket.

"Let me," I murmur.

Lust vibrates in the space between us as I reach

for his tie, my fingers working the knot. I'm about to drop it onto the floor, but he stops me, yanking it from my grasp. A devilish grin curls on his mouth.

"Let's keep this handy." He dips his head into the crook of my neck, nipping my skin. "You never know when I might need to restrain you. Or blindfold you."

My core clenches as desire pools between my thighs. I crane my head, inviting his intoxicating touch to explore further. His hands move along my frame, teasing me with each subtle caress.

But I need more than just his hands. I need all of him.

Pushing against him, I swiftly unbutton his shirt and shove it down his arms, discarding it onto the floor. His socks and pants soon join it, his erection springing free. I wrap my hand around it, my thumb spreading the pre-cum around his tip, eliciting a groan.

"Goddamn, Parker." He grips my face, his breathing ragged. "What the hell are you doing to me?"

"The same thing you're doing to me," I admit honestly.

He slams his lips back to mine as I continue sliding my hand up and down his length, relishing in the tiny groans of pleasure I elicit from him.

"My turn," he growls after several seconds, stepping out of my touch.

"Your turn?" I repeat, my brow arched.

Biting his lower lip, he gives me a slow nod, danger flashing in his dark eyes.

"To undress you." He spins me around and pushes my hair over one shoulder.

He lowers the zipper of my dress with a tantalizing slowness that sets me ablaze, caressing every inch of me as he slides the material off my body, allowing it to pool at my feet.

But he doesn't let me face him. Not yet. Instead, he loops an arm around my waist and forces me against him, my back to his front. God, what I wouldn't give for him to bend me over this bed and take me from behind. To feel him drive into me. To succumb to all the things he makes me feel.

But I want this more. This intoxicating dance of seduction.

His lips float over my skin, traveling from my nape and down my spine. When his fingertips graze my hipbone, skimming the line of my panties, I let out a low moan.

"Please," I beg.

"Please what?" Callum croons, his free hand finding the clasp of my bra and undoing it.

"Please…anything. I need to feel you. Need you to make me feel."

"And I plan on it." His voice oozes with lust as he

drops my bra onto the floor. "But I need you to do something for me in return."

"What's that?"

He scoops his tie off the mattress and brings it up to my face. "Trust me?" he murmurs into my ear.

"Yes," I exhale.

I'll agree to anything if it means I can feel him sooner.

"Good girl."

A shiver rushes through me, a visceral reaction to him calling me his good girl. I doubt I'll ever tire of hearing it.

Although this very well could be the last time I ever do.

Callum secures the fabric around my head, and my world immediately goes dark, heightening the rest of my senses.

The sound of my racing heart as I stand completely exposed, unsure what to expect.

The smell of him as he circles me, as if I'm a sculpture and he a discerning critic.

The feel of him as he runs a lithe finger down my jawline, causing my teeth to chatter.

Then the taste of him as his lips cover mine, his tongue tempting. Demanding. Captivating.

With a hand on my hip, he guides me toward the bed and lowers me onto it. His facial hair scrapes on my skin as he moves down my body, wrapping his mouth around a nipple.

I arch my back and thread my fingers through his hair, encouraging him to keep going. And that's precisely what he does. He worships one nipple. Then the other. Then travels down my stomach, kissing every inch of me until he settles between my thighs.

I lift my hips, expecting for him to take off my panties.

"No. I want you like this."

"Like what?"

He presses a hand to my stomach, gluing me to the mattress, limiting my movement. "Like this."

He covers my panties with his mouth, eliciting a noiseless gasp from my throat. This is torture. Not only is he restricting my movements, but there's a barrier between us when I'd give anything to feel his lips on me.

As if sensing my need, he slips a finger under my panties, spreading my slickness around. But he still keeps my underwear in place as he presses his mouth back against me.

"I can feel how wet you are through your panties, Parker. How desperate you are for me."

"I am," I moan. "I need your tongue on me, Callum. Please."

"No. I want you to come in your panties." He

slides a finger inside me, exploring and stretching. "Need a souvenir to take with me."

If feeling him thrust a finger inside as he returns his mouth to me isn't enough, knowing he plans to take my panties with him sends a rush of excitement through me. If he wants these as a souvenir, who am I to disappoint?

"God, I love this cunt," he rasps, increasing his ministrations as he eases yet another finger inside. "Love how tight you are. Love how fucking delicious you are."

"Callum," I whimper, the combination of his words and fingers propelling me higher.

"Let go, Parker. I need you to come for me."

"Your tongue. Need it on my clit."

I can feel his smile without seeing it. "And I'll always give you what you need." He slides my panties to the side and drags his tongue along my clit before sucking it into his mouth.

"Fuck. That's it."

I try to circle my hips, but his hand on my stomach limits my motions, leaving me completely at his mercy.

He sucks harder. Finger fucks me faster. Nibbles on my clit a little more.

My breathing increases, my insides burning as I fight against my release, wanting to prolong this. But it's impossible with someone as talented as Callum.

Soon, I'm crying out his name as my body convulses. Even when he slips my panties over me and covers them with his mouth, it's still an incredible sensation, the warmth against the material extending my bliss.

Once my aftershocks have finally subsided, he lifts my hips and slides my panties down my legs. I hear some rustling in the room, then feel the bed dip.

His lips are on mine at the same time as he rips off my blindfold, giving me a taste of him and me in one addictive combination. I wrap my legs around his waist, moaning when I feel his erection against my clit.

"Do you want me to fuck you?"

"Yes."

"Do you want my cock?"

I shudder, his words alone unraveling me more than I thought possible after my last orgasm. But that's one thing I've learned during my time with Callum. Anything's possible.

"Say it, Parker. Tell me you want my cock." He nips along the column of my throat. "Tell me you want me to fuck you. Tell me how desperate your greedy cunt is for me."

"I am, Callum. So desperate. Need you to fuck me. Need your cock inside me."

"I love hearing you say that." He crashes his mouth against mine, and I dig my fingers into his hair, savoring every swipe of his tongue, every clash of our teeth, every circle of his hips.

When he eases inside of me, I gasp, but he doesn't stop kissing me. And I don't want him to. Want to wring every last ounce of pleasure I can out of him.

"God, baby," he exhales, closing his eyes as bliss rolls over his expression. "You feel so damn good." He locks his gaze on mine. "How do you feel so damn good? How do you make me feel like this?"

"Like what?" I pant.

"Like I've lost all control."

"Then do it, Callum." I tighten my hold on him. "Lose control. One last time."

"One last time," he grunts.

But he doesn't increase his motions.

Instead, he rocks his hips sensually against me as he holds my face in his hands.

I almost wish he would fuck me harder. That he would put the blindfold back on.

Then I wouldn't have to stare into his eyes as I give him yet another piece of myself.

A piece I know I'll never get back.

And maybe that's okay. Maybe he needs it more than I do.

I drag my nails down his spine, pulling him closer. Fire heats my veins as he buries his head in my neck, his tiny groans and whimpers of pleasure overwhelming me. I tighten my legs around him, rolling my hips in time with him.

His rhythm increases and he pulls back, trapping me in his eyes, making it impossible to look away. Ecstasy unfurls inside me at the same time as he shudders, the only soundtrack to our release that of my uneven breathing and breaking heart.

TWENTY-EIGHT

Callum

Pale golden light creeps through the curtains, illuminating the room with a soft glow. I want to curse the sun for rising before I'm ready.

Then again, I doubt I'll ever truly be ready for what today will bring.

As I admire Parker's slumbering form, I swallow down a renewed wave of emotion, reminding myself this is for the best. I'm better off if I keep all my relationships superficial.

But nothing about my time with Parker has been superficial. Instead, it's been more meaningful than I ever intended.

I pull her close, peppering kisses along her shoulders. It doesn't matter how many times I had her last night. How many times I lost myself in the things she makes me feel. I need her one more time.

I fear I always will.

I move my hand up to her breast, squeezing a nipple. She whimpers, slowly circling her hips, the feel of her ass against my erection causing it to harden and throb. I nibble at her nape, savoring in her taste. In her scent. In her everything.

"I need you, Parker," I rasp, my voice husky from sleep.

"I'm yours."

I squeeze my eyes shut. It's not the first time she's said this. But it's the first time it causes a pang of regret to wrap around me. I know if I asked, she would be mine.

"Mine," I grunt, smoothing my hand down her stomach and toying with her clit.

"Yours." She props her leg up, allowing me better access. But I don't want her like this. If this is to be our last time together, I need to look into her eyes. Need to relish every gasp, every quiver, every moan.

I push her onto her back and settle between her legs, staring into her sparkling blue eyes. I still remember the first time I peered into them. Remember being surprised Parker Holley was a woman, a breathtakingly beautiful one at that.

As I've gotten to know her — learned why this place is so important to her, all the good she's done

not just for her employees but also the community —
she's only become more beautiful.

I smooth a few strands of hair out of her face, my
lips descending toward hers. When they meet, I
moan, drawing in her breath and taking it as my own.
My tongue caresses hers, exploring her mouth for
what will be one of the last times.

Her legs wrap around me, her heat against my
erection a welcome invitation. Pulling back, I lock my
eyes with hers as I bring my arousal up to her. She
doesn't look away, doesn't even blink as I ease inside
her. Slow. Measured. Deliberate.

When I'm in as deep as I can go, I release a shud-
dering breath, a shiver rolling over my body at just
how amazing she feels. Nothing has ever felt this
incredible. This fulfilling. This consuming.

I cover her body with mine, our fingers inter-
locking as I move inside her. There are no heavy
pants. No lustful words. Instead, I keep her hands
enclosed in mine, our eyes unwavering as we chase
our bliss one last time.

An awkward silence settles between us as we leave the
cottage, making the sound of my suitcase scraping
along the dirt path all that more noticeable.

A taunting reminder that I'm leaving.

Parker had planned on slipping out before the sun rose, like she normally does. I was the one who insisted she stay. Told her I wanted to wake up with her in my arms. That I wanted to enjoy every last second with her.

Now, a part of me wishes I hadn't. This would have been much easier if we'd just gone our separate ways in the predawn hours.

"I hope you enjoyed your stay at Holley Ridge, Mr. Reed," Parker says once we reach the parking lot.

"I certainly did." I come to a stop and face her. "Particularly the deluxe package."

She laughs, and I'm grateful for the break in tension. But it only lasts a second before her expression falls, sadness shadowing her features. Her brow furrows and tears well in her eyes, which she quickly blinks away.

Without thinking, I take her face in my hands and touch my lips to hers. She whimpers, the sound a cross between a sob and a moan as I kiss her for the last time.

When I reluctantly bring our exchange to an end, I rest my forehead on hers, drawing in a deep breath.

This shouldn't be so hard. I've entered this kind of arrangement before. Hell, since Sadie, it's the only kind of relationship I've had.

The only kind of intimacy I've been interested in.

But Parker changed all that. Made me question everything.

Made me want things I haven't in a long time. Things I didn't think I'd ever want again.

And that fucking petrifies me.

Releasing her, I fix my expression, rebuilding the wall around my heart Parker all but decimated this week, brick by heavy brick.

"I'll reach out after the holiday to see where you stand on this property."

I allow myself one last look at her before turning and heading toward my rental car. Every voice in my head urges me to stop. That I'm making a mistake. That if I get in the car and drive away, I'll regret it for the rest of my life.

But I'll regret allowing her into my heart and having her obliterate it more.

"So that's it?"

Her tone forces me to stop. I hesitate for a beat then glance over my shoulder. "What do you mean?"

She advances toward me and I fully face her. "This." She gestures between our bodies. "You're really okay with it ending?"

"I told you I couldn't give you more than this week. You said you were okay with that."

"I thought I was." She pulls her lips between her teeth, briefly floating her eyes to the sky, attempting to get her emotions under control. "But what if you're the solution I asked for?"

I blink repeatedly. "What are you talking about?"

The wind blows around us, kicking up her familiar scent of apples and cinnamon. And me. My mark has been left on her. I shouldn't like it as much as I do.

"I'm talking about manifestation. I know you think it's crazy, that you can't just put something out into the universe and expect it to give you what you want. But what if you being here is the universe giving me what I need?"

"I don't—"

"I wasn't going to say anything. I had every intention of just letting you walk away and focusing on what's important. Or what I *thought* was important.

"But maybe I've been wrong about all of it. I've been fighting and fighting to save this place. To save Christmas. To save my memories of my parents. But in doing so, I've been clinging to the past. Been living in it. Maybe you coming into my life and making me feel things I didn't think possible is the universe telling me it's okay to let go of the past."

She grabs my hand in hers, and electricity courses through me from the contact, despite both of our hands being covered with gloves.

"And maybe it's okay for *you* to let go of the past, too."

My chest squeezes, emotion welling in my throat.

I want to give her the answer she deserves more than anything. But I've been here before.

Gave my heart to someone, only for them to completely decimate it.

Sadie and I had planned our life together. I'd started a damn baby book, wrote letters to my unborn child I planned to share with him when he was older. Bought onesies that said Daddy's Little Sidekick. Spent hours designing the perfect nursery.

And all along, Sadie knew I wasn't the father.

I can't put myself through that again.

Won't put myself through that again.

"We agreed," I say, the uncertainty in my voice betraying me. "One week. Nothing more."

I start to turn from her, but before I can, she advances on me again.

"Why, Callum? Give me one good reason why you refuse to give us a chance and I'll walk away and never look back. But I need a reason." She lifts her tear-filled eyes to mine. "Please. I think you owe me that much."

I want to tell her I don't owe her anything. But some outside force takes over, pushing me to finally give voice to my biggest fears.

"Because I can't stomach the thought of losing you like I did Sadie," I admit through the unbearable ache consuming me.

My entire body vibrates with every single emotion

I've kept buried for the past week. Hell, for the past several years.

"Because I can't deal with the idea of planning a life with you, only for it not to work out in the end. Because I know it'll be a hundred times worse based on the crazy way I've—" I stop short.

"With the way you've what, Callum?" she presses, touching her hand to my arm, not allowing me to escape this.

I blow out a long sigh. "The way I've fallen for you."

"You say it like it's a bad thing." She reaches for my cheek, but I push out of her hold before I can fall under her spell again.

"It is, Parker. It's the worst thing that's happened to me in a long time. I need certainties. Absolutes." I shake my head. "And feelings? They're too unpredictable."

"So you're not even going to try?" she shouts, throwing up her hands in frustration. "You're not even going to take a risk, knowing it could work out and be the best thing that's ever happened to you?"

I want to. My god, do I want to.

But every time I even consider it, I remember staring at the 3D ultrasound of what I thought was my baby's face as I watched Sadie pack her things and walk out of the house where I thought we'd build a family.

A lone tear slides down my cheek, but I quickly swipe it away. "I can't."

"Can't?" She sucks in a shuttering breath. "Or won't?"

I bring my hands to her arms, touching my lips to her forehead. "I'm sorry." I linger for several long moments.

Then I pull back, continuing to my car and placing my suitcase in the back.

"I'm not her, ya' know," Parker calls out just as I'm about to slide behind the wheel.

"What's that?" I glance her way.

"I'm not Sadie. You've spent the past few years keeping people away because of what she did to you. And I get it. But you know what they say, don't you?"

I swallow hard, remaining silent.

"The best revenge is living well. You may have millions in your bank account, but we both know money is just colored paper. Are you really living well?"

She holds my gaze, her question twisting around me, taunting and tormenting. Then she turns, her steps determined as she stomps across the parking lot and disappears inside the inn.

I should chase her. Tell her she's right. That I haven't been living well.

But I don't.

Instead, I get into the car and do the only thing I can.

I leave.

TWENTY-NINE

Parker

A melancholy feeling clings to the air as I trudge down the snow-lined path toward the playground, mentally preparing myself to answer all of Haley's prodding questions about how it went with Callum.

A part of me hoped he'd change his mind. That he'd get to the edge of the parking lot and realize he made a mistake, slam on his brakes, and hurry inside, sweeping me into his arms and declaring his devotion.

That never happened.

Instead, whenever I stole a glimpse of the cottage, my heart broke a little more.

I knew there was a chance he'd respond this way. He has valid reasons for avoiding commitments. Hell, he went so far as to get a vasectomy because of what Sadie and his brother put him through.

Still, there was a tiny part of me that hoped I was wrong.

And now I'll have to rehash the entire thing with Haley while the sting of his rejection is still a fresh wound.

At least, that's what I expect.

But as I sit beside her, I notice she's wearing a forlorn expression of her own, her eyes following Maggie as she zigzags around the playground.

"Penny for your thoughts." I hand Haley a paper cup of coffee that she happily takes.

"She's so happy. Isn't she?"

"The happiest. But that's to be expected." I nudge her. "She's got a great mom."

She pinches her lips into a tight line, and her chin quivers. "I try to be, Parker. But it's definitely not easy, especially lately. Don't get me wrong," she adds quickly. "I'm blessed to have you and Grandma Estelle ready to drop everything at a moment's notice and help with her."

"Because we love that little girl. And you."

"I know, but sometimes I feel so alone. Like no matter what I do, it's not good enough."

She turns her attention back to Maggie, admiring her daughter for several long moments before breaking the silence.

"I talked to him."

"Who?"

"Beckham. Asked about renting his townhouse."

"What did he say?"

"What I expected him to. That his place is booked solid with all the snow bunnies coming here to ski. But then…"

"Yes?" I lean closer.

"He asked me to marry him."

"He…*what?*"

Of all the things that could have come out of her mouth, this was the last thing I expected.

"Took me by surprise, too."

"Aren't people supposed to date before a proposal? At the very least, they have a hot and heavy one-night stand, then plan to never see each other again until those two little lines appear on a pregnancy test, at which point he decides to do the right thing and proposes." My eyes widen as I suck in a gasp. "Oh my god. Did you sleep together? Are you pregnant?"

"Of course not!" Haley insists. "I haven't slept with anyone since I learned I was pregnant with Maggie."

"And you were giving me shit for not dating." I roll my eyes.

"It's not that I don't want to date. I just have other things to take into consideration."

"And yet you're considering marrying Beckham Lawrence?"

"No. Hell, I don't know…" She slumps into the bench.

"Why does he want to marry you?"

"He doesn't *want* to marry me."

"But you said—"

"Grady is planning to sell the vineyard. Beckham made an offer, but Grady's worried he'll make the vineyard his life if he sells to him."

"So he wants him to get married?"

She shrugs. "It appears so."

I take a moment to process all of this. When I came out here to talk to Haley, I assumed she wanted to hound me for details regarding how things went with Callum. I never could have imagined she'd tell me Beckham Lawrence had proposed some sort of marriage of convenience.

"What are your thoughts on his proposition?" I ask.

"It's definitely an attractive offer. Not only will he give me a place to live, but he'll cover all my bills and put Maggie and me on his health insurance. I won't have to worry about anything, so all the money I make—"

"You can use to focus on your cake business," I finish, all too familiar with Haley's true passion.

"Exactly."

"And how long would this fake marriage last?" I ask after a brief moment of contemplation.

"He'd like to stay married for at least six months after the sale is finalized so Grady doesn't feel like he was tricked or lied to. We *would* be tricking him, but it's for a good purpose, I suppose."

"And Maggie?"

"I can't tell her the truth. She'd blab it all over the county. I probably shouldn't even be telling you, since this only works if the entire town believes we're madly in love."

"That won't be a problem." I snort. "Pretty sure there's a pool going for how much longer it'll take before the two of you just bang it out already. You'd have to be blind not to see the chemistry between you two."

"Maggie's where it gets sticky," she responds, ignoring my remark. "It's one thing if we only have to pretend to be married in public, but since I have a four-year-old, I can't have her telling everyone mommy's only married so her fake husband can buy the winery. Which means she needs to believe it's real. Which also means—"

"She'll believe it's real when you split."

Haley nods gravely. "The reason I didn't go after paternity or support from Oliver is because I didn't want Maggie to deal with that kind of rejection or abandonment." She sucks in her lower lip, her voice strained. "I'm not sure if I can put her through that."

"Is it Maggie you're worried about?" I narrow my gaze on her. "Or yourself?"

She opens and shuts her mouth several times, her silence betraying her.

"Enough about me and my problems." She straightens, her voice brightening. "How did it go with Mr. Sex in a Suit?"

I'm about to call her out for purposefully changing the subject, but after this morning, I don't have it in me. "It didn't."

She tilts her head. "You didn't tell him how you feel?"

"I did." I give her a sad smile. "But it wasn't enough."

"Oh, Parker..." She wraps an arm around me and pulls me closer. "I'm sorry, sweetie."

"It's okay. Like Mama always said, everyone comes into our lives for a reason."

"And what was the reason for him?"

"That maybe it's time to move on. Keep the past in the past."

"Are you sure?" she asks, knowing exactly what I'm referring to. "I thought you were holding out for a miracle."

I swallow hard through the lump building in my throat as I rest my head on Haley's shoulder.

"I'm starting to think the universe might be all out of miracles."

THIRTY

Callum

Heavy fog blurs the bustling city surrounding me, clinging in thick sheets to the San Francisco skyline. Thirty-seven stories below, locals and tourists swarm the streets, soaking in the final few days of holiday cheer before Santa's big night. White lights outline the trees, wreaths decorating the street lamps. Even the famous San Francisco cable cars are decked out with reminders of the season.

I hate it.

But for a different reason than I did just a few weeks ago.

Now every tree, every light, every snowman reminds me of Parker Holley.

Her laugh.

Her smile.

Her heart.

And it makes me ache.

Makes me second-guess my decision.

But every time I debate hopping on the next flight so I can grovel at Parker's feet, I'm reminded how I felt after learning the truth about my brother and Sadie. Watching her walk out of our house and into Mason's idling car. Staring at all the presents beneath the Christmas tree meant for the son I'd soon meet, only to learn he wasn't mine at all.

The only reason I survived without drowning in a bottle is because I had my work. I turned my crushing heartbreak into something else. Something I'm proud of.

I'd convinced myself this was all I needed. That my work made me happy.

And it did.

Not once over the past few years have I ever felt like something was missing. I get to travel the world. Experience things most people never will. See my vision for abandoned pieces of property come to life.

Now, as I stare at the blueprints my team sent over for the potential development of Holley Ridge, it feels wrong.

Everything has since I drove away from Parker.

"Are those the blueprints?"

I snap my head up as Daniel strolls into my office,

his casual attire of jeans and a button-down shirt at odds with my crisp suit and tie. His complexion is darker than it was the last time I saw him, the ends of his brown hair tinged blond. It's obvious he spent a fair bit of time in the sun while on his honeymoon.

"They are," I tell him.

"And what's the status? Do you need me to head out there? Smooth things over with the property owner?"

I push out a breath, unsure how to respond. He assumes I was an unforgivable asshole to Parker.

I guess I kind of was.

I doubt any smoothing over Daniel does will fix this. I knew I shouldn't have slept with her, not with the property sale at stake. Now, not only do I feel like a shitty human for how I treated her, but I also have nothing to show for it.

"There's something you should know…"

"Uh oh." Daniel pushes out an anxious laugh. "This doesn't sound good. How bad did you screw things up? What kind of damage control will I have to do? I told you to be nice. See her as a person and not just someone standing between you and adding several zeroes to your bank account."

"And I did that. But I think I may have—"

"Excuse me, Mr. Reed," my assistant interrupts, peeking her head into my office.

I wave her in, and she walks toward my desk,

smiling at Daniel before returning her attention to me.

"This was just delivered by courier." She places an overnight envelope on the edge of my desk. "Figured you'd want to know right away, considering the return address."

As I pick it up, my eyes fixate on the familiar address of Holley Ridge in Sycamore Falls, and a pang squeezes my heart. I quickly push it down, my face becoming a mask of indifference.

"Thank you, Dakota."

"Is that what I hope it is?" Daniel asks once we're alone.

"I don't know." I flip over the envelope, but don't immediately rip it open. A part of me hopes it isn't.

Parker was adamant about not signing anything until after Christmas in the hopes of a miracle.

The idea that she's given up on her miracle stings more than learning Sadie had been cheating on me with my own brother.

Because this time, I'm the one to blame.

Swallowing hard, I peel back the seal and remove the contents. On the very top of the short stack of papers is a handwritten note. I run my fingers over Parker's familiar script, resisting the urge to bring the paper to my face to see if it carries her scent.

Mr. Reed,

Enclosed, you'll find a signed acceptance of your offer to buy the parcel of land commonly referred to as Holley Ridge. This will conclude our business relationship. If you need anything further, please direct your inquiries to my attorney. Her business card is attached. She's authorized to act fully on my behalf.

Sincerely,

Parker Holley

I don't know what I expected. But the curt and professional tone in her letter leaves me unsettled. They're just words. I receive hundreds of letters such as this every week.

But they may as well be in the shape of a knife for how much they gut me.

I flip through the papers, my heart sinking more with each page containing her initials in the corner. When I reach the final one and see her signature neatly scribbled on the line, my shoulders deflate.

This is what I wanted.

So why do I feel so shitty?

"Looks like you did it after all," Daniel says jovially, rising from his chair and skirting around my desk.

In a daze, I stand, and he gives me a short bro-hug before walking over to the wet bar, pouring some scotch into a couple of rocks glasses. Returning to the desk, he hands me one. I stare into space as he clinks his glass against mine. But I don't take a sip. This doesn't feel like a celebration.

"Oh, fuck."

I dart my eyes toward Daniel. "What?"

He rakes his analytical gaze over me, scrutinizing me in a way only my best friend could.

"Tell me something, Callum..." He plops back down into his chair, resting his ankle on his opposite knee, completely relaxed.

Then again, he's always relaxed. It's why people feel comfortable around him. Why he's so good at what he does. He's personable. Approachable. Doesn't walk around with a chip on his shoulder.

"Before Dakota came in, you were telling me that you took my advice and were friendly to Ms. Holley. But then you started saying something else. That you may have...what?"

On a long exhale, I slump into my chair and take a few gulps of the scotch, savoring the warmth as it slides down my throat. "I think I may have gotten to know her *too* well."

"I see." It's silent for a moment while he processes this. "By the forlorn look on your face, I'm guessing it didn't end all that amicably."

"It was supposed to. We agreed from the beginning we'd walk away when my reservation ended. That way, we wouldn't complicate things."

Daniel barks out a laugh. "The second you sleep with someone, it gets complicated, despite what you want to believe. Let me guess. She decided she wanted more and you, being who you are, told her you couldn't, all because of Sadie."

"I don't have time for a relationship. Not with this project officially on our plate now." I swallow hard through the sour taste in my mouth over the idea.

"And if it wasn't this project, it would be a different one. Or some other excuse."

"It's not an excuse. People depend on me."

"People depend on me, too, yet I found time to date. To fall in love. To get married."

"I've...dated."

Daniel gives me a skeptical look. "I'm not sure I'd count the occasional one-night stand as dating."

"I travel a lot."

"So do I."

"But I—"

"Listen, Callum," he interrupts before I can make yet another bullshit argument.

At this point, he's heard them all.

"I get why you're the way you are."

"And how *am* I?" I ask hesitantly, unsure I want to hear his response.

"Scared."

"I'm not scared," I insist, but don't look directly at him.

"Mason was a bastard for what he did. Sadie, too. I didn't say anything when the shit hit the fan because I figured you needed time to sort it all out. But it's been three years now. You need to stop living this half-life because you're too scared of having a repeat of Sadie. That's why you work every waking hour. Somewhere in your head, you think if you work all the time and make as much money as possible, it'll make up for the part of your life that's lacking."

"And what's that?" I snip out.

"The important things, Cal. Someone to share your life with. Friends. Family. Hell, I'd be happy if you'd get a fucking goldfish at this point. Did you learn nothing from *A Christmas Carol?* You can have all the zeroes you want in your bank account, but what good is it if you don't have anyone to share it with?"

"I tried that once. It didn't exactly work out."

"Because she wasn't the one." He takes another sip of his drink, a contemplative look crossing his brow. "Remember when you asked me if I believed in manifestation or the law of attraction?"

"Yes…," I draw out.

"I think there's a reason you stumbled on this particular parcel of land. Call it fate. Call it destiny. I don't care. But it's obvious this woman made you think." He punches the signed acceptance with his finger. "And maybe, just maybe, the universe made sure you were the one to convince her to sell for a reason other than adding a few zeroes to your bank account. Hannah always says the universe gives us what we need when we need it. Maybe that's what happened here."

I heave a long sigh and shake my head.

While I appreciate that Daniel cares about me enough to want me to be happy, there's still one problem.

"I hurt her. Made her give up on her miracle."

"Her…miracle?"

"She told me she wouldn't consider my offer until after Christmas. Claimed she couldn't give up hoping for a miracle. So this…" I flip through the signed offer. "It means she gave up hope."

"Then you need to do something to restore that hope." He drains the rest of his glass and stands.

"Like what?"

He shrugs. "That's for you to figure out. But if I were you, I'd start with tearing this up." He pushes the offer across the desk toward me.

"Are you sure?" I stand, eyes narrowed. "You'd make a fortune, Daniel."

"It's only money." He feigns choking on his words, as if struggling to say them. "I'd rather my best friend be happy. Does she make you happy?"

"More than I thought possible," I admit, much to my surprise.

"Then go after that. We can always make more money on a different project. But there may never be another Parker Holley. It's just a question of what's more important to you." He arches a brow, waiting for my response.

I don't even have to think about it. For the first time in my life, I know precisely what that is. And it's nothing in this city.

Spinning from him, I shove my laptop into my bag and grab my coat, practically running out of my office.

"Good answer, Cal."

THIRTY-ONE

Parker

Fluffy white snowflakes fall from the sky as I walk through Holley Ridge, savoring the sights and smells of the Christmas festival. A raw ache settles in my chest with the knowledge that this time next year, this place will look vastly different. No rows of vendors selling holiday crafts. No North Pole where kids can visit Santa. No ice rink where people of all ages can skate with snow falling around them.

I pray the tree remains. I hate the idea of this Norway spruce being chopped down to make room for more luxury timeshares.

As much as I didn't want to give up on my ranch, I need to be realistic. And the reality is the chance of some miracle happening, allowing me to pay off my debts on this property, is non-existent.

Haley and Grandma Estelle asked if I was only doing this because of how things ended between Callum and me.

I'm not.

Just like I knew how it would always end between us, I knew this was how it would end for Holley Ridge.

At least I'll no longer have the stress hanging over me and I can enjoy my last Christmas here.

"So what are you going to do?" Bernie asks as I stroll past the veranda, the unofficial Holley Ridge chess club focused on their matches.

All except Bernie, who is sadly without a partner now that Callum's gone.

"What do you mean?"

"Once the sale goes through. What are your plans? You staying in Sycamore Falls?"

The truth is, I have no idea. Nearly every night since I signed those papers, I've snuggled up on my couch with a glass of wine and my journal, trying to make a list of what I should do.

The page is still blank.

Haley insists it's a sign I shouldn't have sold. Not yet anyway.

But I think I'm done believing in signs.

I pull my coat tighter and shrug. "I'm not sure.

There won't be much reason for me to stay anymore. I'll miss everyone, but I don't know…" I blink back the tears threatening to fall.

As much as I love the town I've called home for most of my life, I'm not sure I can stay. Not sure I can bear watching my family home be demolished and resurrected as luxury homes for the ski bunnies.

Not sure I can stand a daily reminder of my biggest failure.

And my biggest mistake.

"I don't know if I can stay."

Bernie doesn't push. Doesn't prod. Doesn't tell me I'm not only making a mistake in leaving but also in selling. There's nothing but acceptance and understanding in his eyes.

"Your father would have been proud. If he were here, he would have done the same thing. Not just in deciding to sell, but what you did to help your employees during those difficult years. I'm sure he's looking down on you right now and smiling."

"Thanks, Bernie."

"You bet, kid. Now come on." He motions for me to join him. "I could use a partner."

I hesitate, surveying the large crowds of people coming through Holley Ridge.

"If you could take a break from work to have relations with Callum, you can humor an old man with a game of chess."

I push down the embarrassment that Bernie, one of my father's best friends, just called me out for "having relations" with Callum. I suppose it's better than using one of Grandma Estelle's colorful terms. I'd probably die of embarrassment if he accused me of skipping out on work to play hide the sausage.

"For old time's sake," he encourages. "I remember when you used to run home from school just so we could get in a game of chess before your riding lesson."

"Okay." I climb onto the veranda, saying a quick hello to the other chess players before sitting across from Bernie.

I wait for him to make the first move, since he's playing the white pieces. Instead, he huffs out an annoyed breath.

"Damn bladder." He pushes to his feet. "Excuse me a moment, dear."

"Of course."

He retreats, using his cane to hobble along the veranda and inside the inn, leaving me alone with my thoughts.

I try to find comfort in Bernie's assurances that my dad would have made the same decision I did. That he'd be proud of me. That he wouldn't wish he'd left his family's property to someone more deserving.

As I look at all the crowds swarming the ridge, I

think maybe he's right, especially when I take into account all the happy memories people made because of this place. All the marriages that began here. Hell, I'm pretty sure quite a few families were started in the hotel rooms here, too.

Holley Ridge may soon be gone, but its legacy will continue, regardless of anything Callum Reed may do.

I'm so lost in my thoughts, I don't realize how much time has passed until I hear footsteps approach from behind.

But they can't belong to Bernie. There's no unsteady rhythm of his cane.

A prickle of awareness cascades down my spine, a familiar woodsy scent invading my senses. Snapping my head up, I inhale a sharp breath as my eyes lock on Callum Reed.

He looks just as handsome as he did the day we met. Wool coat. Red scarf. An unshaven jawline that brings back memories of how incredible it felt scraping between my thighs.

But there's something different about him, too. Something...off.

I'd expected for him to be thrilled I finally accepted his offer.

Instead, he looks...sad. Morose.

Empty.

I scramble to my feet, smoothing a hand down my

coat. "Mr. Reed. I specifically told you to reach out to my attorney should you require anything further in regards to our agreement."

"That *is* what you wrote. But when I was reviewing the offer, I realized I wanted to make a few changes."

"Like I said, my attorney—"

"I know what you said. But before I propose these changes, I need an answer."

"Again, you can reach out to my attorney. She's authorized to act on my behalf."

"Not about this, she's not."

I shake my head. "I don't know what—"

"Did you mean it?" he interrupts before I can utter another syllable. The anguish in his tone gives me pause, my heart squeezing.

"Mean what?"

He takes a step toward me, and then another, bridging the gap between us until our bodies are practically touching.

"The other morning, you said that maybe the universe *did* give you the solution you needed. That maybe *I* was the solution."

I avert my gaze. "I don't see how that matters anymore."

"It matters to me, Parker. So please…," he chokes out. "I need to know. At the time, did you really believe the universe made our paths cross as a sign you should stop living in the past?"

The last thing I want to do is relive this all over again. But something about the vulnerability in his eyes has me responding when I'd love nothing more than to escape.

As if the universe knows I need to be here.

That we need to have this conversation.

"I did, but—"

"I do, too."

I snap my mouth shut, his words stealing my breath. "You...*do*?"

"Yes. Well, kind of."

"Kind of?"

"You asked the universe for a miracle." He shrugs, giving me a sheepish smile. "Maybe that's me." He reaches into his coat and retrieves a few papers, extending them toward me.

I almost don't want to take them. Don't want to allow myself to feel anything for him again, only for him to refuse to let me in. But when my eyes fall on the pages, I suck in a sharp inhale.

"What is this, Callum?" I ask with a quiver, taking them from him, the words not registering. It doesn't make sense.

Why would he do this?

"I ran some numbers based on past and projected

revenue. This is an offer to buy twenty-three percent of the shares in Holley Ridge. If you'll turn to the last page, that sum equals all outstanding debts on this property."

My heart races as I frantically flip through the pages.

"Of course, you'll see I'm not hoping to acquire any managerial duties or board positions. I'll be more of…an angel investor. I'll provide you with enough capital to get back on your feet. But the day-to-day running of this property will remain under your sole authority."

I blink repeatedly, still not understanding.

"Why?" I meet his gaze, my brow creased. "Don't you stand to make millions off all the timeshares you plan to build?"

"I prefer to have a diverse portfolio."

"Is that the only reason you're doing this? To diversify your portfolio?"

He slowly shakes his head, lifting his hand toward me. When his fingertips graze my cheek, I don't back away.

"I've also realized there are more important things than money. Than my work."

"Like what?"

He brings his other hand to my face, cupping my cheeks in his firm grasp, the roughness of his skin invigorating.

"You, Parker. You're more important than any of

it. I'm sorry I was such a damn idiot. The other day, you said the best revenge is living well. You're right. I haven't been living well. Hell, until you walked into my life, I wasn't even living. But I want to."

His lips slowly descend toward mine, his breath kissing my mouth, causing a shiver to rush through me.

"I want to live with you. Want to dream with you. Want it all with you. If you'll have me." He swipes away the few tears that have escaped, nothing but raw, unfiltered honesty filling his eyes. "And I *really* hope you will, Parker. More than I want my next breath."

When I first met Callum, I didn't think he was capable of sharing his feelings with such candor. He was so cold, uncaring, aloof. But after learning why he was this way, it made sense. I understood why he'd erected an unscalable wall around his heart.

But for some reason, I was able to climb it.

Better yet, he was willing to let me in when he's made a habit of keeping people out.

I'd be crazy to keep him out now.

"You know…" I drape an arm over his shoulder, toying with a few tendrils of hair that hang over his collar. "That's an unusually romantic thing to say for someone who I didn't think had any knowledge of the concept."

"I can do romance. I just haven't been with someone I felt the need to. Not in a long while." For the first time, his expression doesn't fall at the reminder of Sadie. Instead, his eyes gleam with hope.

"And now?"

"Now…" He licks his lips as he dips his head closer. "Now, I find myself feeling things I'd forgotten about."

"Me, too," I sigh, the weight I've been carrying the past few days evaporating. "I'm sorry I—"

"Will you just kiss her already, for crying out loud?"

Callum and I dart our eyes to the right, Bernie and the rest of the chess players watching with bated breath.

Hell, practically everyone is watching us with rapt attention. I hadn't even noticed we'd drawn a crowd. Then again, that's the effect Callum Reed has on me. Whenever I'm with him, he's all I care about.

All that matters.

"I was about to before you interrupted," Callum grits out in mock frustration.

"Well, get on with it already," Harry calls out. "Unless you don't know how."

"Oh, I know how."

"Doesn't look like it," Leonard chimes in. "In my day, we would have already found somewhere more private." He waggles his bushy brow. "If you know what I mean."

"What's it going to be, Mr. Reed?" I tease,

chewing on my lower lip. "Are you going to let them get away with that? Or should you prove you *do* know what you're doing?"

"Gladly, Ms. Holley."

Without another moment of hesitation, he presses his lips against mine, leaving no question in my mind this man absolutely knows what he's doing.

When Callum Reed first showed up at Holley Ridge, I swore to do everything in my power to fight for this place. Prevent him from stealing it. From stealing Christmas.

Never in my wildest imagination could I have anticipated the man who tried to steal Christmas would be the one who ended up saving it.

And in turn, he sort of saved me, too.

"Shall I get you checked in now, Mr. Reed?" I coo as he rests his forehead on mine. "I think you might prefer our elite package this time around, however."

"And what does that include?" His reply drips with sin and seduction.

"All the amenities of the deluxe package, plus the benefit of my personal attention and presence twenty-four/seven."

He nuzzles the crook of my neck. "I like the sound of twenty-four/seven access."

"You'll also be entitled to spa services, complete with frequent rub downs and happy endings."

His pupils dilate, his jaw twitching. "Any other...benefits?"

"Yes. One more."

"And that is?" he growls, his eyes blazing.

I hoist myself onto my toes. "Me. In the elf costume. With no panties."

His hold on me tightens, every muscle in his body going rigid.

Including the one I feel pressing against my stomach, despite the layers between us.

"I'm going to need you to check me in. Effective immediately."

"Of course, sir." I bat my lashes. "And how long do you plan on staying?"

His expression shifts from lustful to sincere. "As long as you'll have me, Parker. I'm yours."

I brush my mouth against his. "And I'm yours."

THIRTY-TWO

Callum

Pride practically bursts out of my chest as I meander through the crowd gathered at Holley Ridge for the annual tree lighting ceremony, shaking hands and giving hugs to all the locals who've become like family over the past year. It's a stark contrast from how I felt during last year's ceremony, standing off to the side, thinking all this Christmas frivolity was excessive and a waste of money. I never could have anticipated being back here this year.

And I certainly never could have anticipated being here because I'm madly in love with the woman who owns it.

Over the past year, I helped Parker realize her dreams of turning this place into a full-service resort while still keeping the charm and individualized service it's known for.

She's not the only one I've helped, either.

Instead of focusing all my efforts and capital on finding properties on the brink of foreclosure and convincing the owner to sell, I've started a second company whose sole mission is to be an angel investor for struggling businesses, much like I did with Parker. Now my days are spent finding businesses in need of a miracle. I give them that miracle.

As long as they have a viable business plan and meet a demand in the community. I'm not about to invest in a clothing line for nudists.

I still have my real estate development firm, but now we're selective in the pieces of property we try to acquire. No more swooping in before foreclosure and convincing someone to part with the land that's been in their family for generations. Not now that I've finally realized the human aspect of these types of situations.

I used to think the mark of success was earning as much money as possible. Success looks different now. It's having a career I can be happy with. That makes me feel fulfilled. And I've never been as fulfilled as I am now.

All thanks to Parker.

She brought me back to life, made me feel again.

She often jokes I was a Grinch when we first met,

that my heart was two sizes too small. There's a kernel of truth to that. And just like the people of Who-ville helped the Grinch's heart grow three sizes, Parker helped my heart grow.

And it still grows every day I'm lucky enough to spend with her.

"There you are."

At the sound of that sweet voice, I snap out of my thoughts and watch Parker saunter toward me. There's something about seeing her in her red wool coat, blonde hair cascading down her back in loose waves, and the red lipstick that steals my breath.

Even after a year.

"Sorry I'm late." I pull her close, tipping her chin back and pressing my lips to hers. "My flight was delayed."

While Parker and I made the decision to move in together earlier in the year, and into a house away from Holley Ridge, forcing her to separate her work life from her home life, I still do travel from time to time.

Not as much as I did before, though. I no longer feel the need to be gone all the time so I don't have to face the fact I'm alone. I'm never alone anymore.

And I couldn't be happier.

"Well, you're here now."

"I am." I wrap my arm around her as she moves to my side, both of us looking out over Holley Ridge.

"It's even more beautiful than I could have imagined," she murmurs.

"It certainly is."

Now that Parker no longer has to worry about how to pay the mortgage on the property, she was able to afford some much needed upgrades to parts of the Christmas festival, some of which were hanging on by a thread.

The North Pole area is bigger than it was in the past and no longer has chipped and faded paint. She even added more decorations all around the lake so people can take an evening stroll and enjoy the lights.

But the best change is that she's been able to delegate more. Instead of trying to do everything herself, she's hired more staff.

Speaking of her staff…

"Who's that with Claire?" I ask, leaning close to her.

She searches the crowd, finding her former front desk employee who she promoted to the head of marketing walking with someone I've never seen before.

It's not unusual, considering the number of people who flock to Holley Ridge this time of year.

But there's something about their body language that tells me they've known each other a while. Which is strange, since I've gotten to know Claire quite well.

Hell, I've gotten to know all the staff at Holley Ridge well. They've become…well, family.

"That's Joshua's dad. Declan."

"Joshua?" I furrow my brow. "You mean our head groundskeeper? That Joshua?"

"They matched on one of those ancestry kits. Isn't that great?"

I glance back at Claire and Declan, studying them for a beat. He's not looking at her like he's her son's friend. And she's not looking at him like he's merely her friend's dad.

"Do you think—"

"Oh, absolutely," Parker interrupts before I can finish my question. "They're totally screwing."

The furrow in my brow only deepens. "But didn't she date Joshua?"

"Yup!" she responds as if it's no big deal. "Shall we? There's still one thing missing."

She grabs my hand, forcing my attention away from Claire and Joshua's father. If they're into each other, who am I to judge? I know what this place can do to people.

I lean down, placing a soft kiss on Parker's head as we make our way through the growing crowd and toward the unlit tree.

While the tree lighting ceremony was well attended last year, there's probably double the amount of people this year. I'm not saying it's because of me.

But once Parker had the resources to hire someone to deal with the financial aspect of running this place, it allowed her to do what she does best. Interact with the guests and make sure their experience here is as enjoyable as possible.

Although, I'm lucky to say I'm the only one who gets to enjoy the elite package.

And I've enjoyed every second of it since I checked back in last December.

And I hope to enjoy it for many years to come.

The choir on the stage serenades the crowd with an *a cappella* rendition of "O Christmas Tree", and Parker and I remain off to the side, taking it all in. Once they finish to enthusiastic applause, I place my hand on the small of her back, leading her up the stairs and to the center of the stage.

As she steps up to the microphone, I stand back, allowing her to have this moment. I didn't even want to be up here. Didn't want to steal her spotlight. But she insisted, claimed none of this would have been possible without me. That I'm a part of Holley Ridge now.

"Thank you so much for being here tonight," she begins, her voice carrying over the crowd. "Last year as I stood in front of all of you, I worried it would be the last time I'd ever be able to do this. But thanks to my very own grump who saved Christmas..." She glances my way with a brilliant smile that melts my heart over again, "we're still here this year. And it's my hope we'll be able to come together every year going forward as all our families grow and we welcome more people to this place that will always hold a special place in my heart.

"But you're not here to listen to me talk. You're here to be the first to see our tree decked out. So without further ado, I give you the Holley Ridge Christmas tree."

She's about to flip the switch to illuminate the tree, but pauses, motioning me over. "You do it."

"Me?"

"None of us would be here if it weren't for you. You deserve this."

I give her a small smile as I walk toward her, touching a soft kiss to her forehead.

When I flick the switch, thousands of twinkling lights illuminate the majestic Norway spruce, stretching from the base all the way to the top where an oversized star glows. The crowd claps enthusiastically as the choir breaks into "The Most Wonderful Time of the Year".

"This is my favorite part," Parker murmurs.

But she's not looking at the tree.

Instead, her attention is focused on all the people assembled. Parents hug children. Couples share a warm embrace. Even brothers and sisters stop rough-housing for a few seconds to admire the tree.

"It's incredible." I face her, cupping her cheeks. "*You're* incredible. Thank you."

"Why are you thanking me?" She laughs. "You're the one who was up in the cherry picker earlier in the week decorating that tree. *I* should be thanking *you*."

"Not that. For letting me be a part of this. And not just tonight, but last year, too. It's been the best year of my life." I curve toward her. "All because of you."

She sighs. "This has been the best year of my life, too. All because of you."

"Then what do you say we keep having the best years? For the rest of our lives. Together. Officially."

She tilts her head. "Officially?"

Before she can utter another syllable, I drop to one knee.

A hush falls over the crowd as I reach into my pocket and remove a small velvet box, displaying a sparkling diamond ring.

The old Callum never would have done something like this in public. Hell, I never would have expressed my feelings like I do around Parker. I doubt I would have even entertained the notion of taking this next step with someone, not wanting to endure what I did with Sadie. It wasn't worth the risk.

But Parker's worth every risk. This past year has taught me that.

"Parker Ellen Holley, before I met you, I'd given

up on love. Happiness. Family. While our beginning certainly wasn't the stuff of fairy tales, I couldn't imagine going through life with anyone else by my side. You make me a better person. A less grumpy person."

She laughs, swiping the few tears that have escaped.

"Because of you, I've started to see the good in life again. With every laugh, every smile, every heartbeat, you've shown me the beauty in this world. Made me believe in miracles. And I'd be honored if you'd spend the rest of your days continuing to show me that miracles can happen, even when you've given up on hope. So please. Be my wife. Let me be your husband. Be my family."

She stares at me for what feels like an eternity, her lips parting as she shakes her head. Then she yanks me to my feet, cupping my face.

"You're so stupid, Callum. You're already *are* my family. You have been since the second you stole my heart."

I pull back, needing to look into her blue eyes. "Is that a yes?"

She grins excitedly. "That's a yes."

I don't waste any time in slamming my lips against hers, the crowd erupting in cheers and applause. I only stop kissing her long enough to slide the ring onto her finger, then press my mouth back to hers. It doesn't matter how many times I've kissed her over the past year. Each one feels like the first. Each one fills me with the same exhilaration and promise.

"I love you, Parker Holley," I murmur once I bring our kiss to an end.

"And I love you, Callum Reed." The corners of her mouth lift slightly, a flirtatious gleam in her eyes. "Perhaps we should discuss upgrading your package here at Holley Ridge."

"Oh, yeah? I quite like the elite package."

"I'm thrilled you've been enjoying all the…benefits."

My eyes flame as I nuzzle her neck. "Have I ever."

"But I think you might enjoy the diamond package better."

"And what's included in that?"

"All the same benefits of the elite package." She licks her lips, a hint of nervousness flashing across her expression. "But it also includes dirty diapers, midnight feedings, and being spit up on."

On a sharp inhale, I stiffen, searching her eyes. "Are you saying…"

She nods. "I am. The doctor confirmed it this morning."

I don't say anything right away, in complete shock. While I had my vasectomy reversed earlier in the year, the doctor said there was a possibility it may not work. It was a smaller chance considering I was only thirty-two when I got it done and it's only been four years. Still, it was possible that even after the reversal, I might not be able to have kids.

Parker said she didn't care. That she wouldn't mind adopting, considering her past.

To hear she's pregnant completely floors me.

Overwhelmed by a love bigger than I thought existed, I crush my mouth against hers, my heart full.

"Is that a yes to the upgrade, Mr. Reed?"

I meet her gaze, sliding my hand to her stomach, my eyes welling with tears. I don't know if I'll ever be able to properly convey just how thankful I am for everything she's given me. But I have the rest of my life to try.

"That's a hell yes."

When I first met Parker and she refused to sell to me because she was manifesting a solution, I thought she was crazy. Thought the only way to get something you needed was by finding a solution yourself. Thought miracles didn't exist.

I was wrong.

Because now I've been gifted with my own Christmas miracle.

I'll never doubt the magic of the season again.

Not ready to leave Holley Ridge just yet? There's more holiday fun in The One Night Stand Before Christmas!

The only thing worse than having a one-night stand with a ridiculously hot stranger during a snowstorm in Boston? Finding out he's your ex-boyfriend's father.

https://getbook.at/OneNightXmas

Wondering how things will fare between Beckham and Haley after his surprising proposal? Find out today in Married to the Frenemy.

He was my first love. My worst heartbreak. And for the next year... My new husband.

https://geni.us/FrenemyTLWeb

Want one last taste of Callum and Parker? Then sign up for my mailing list to get a bonus chapter. Just type in the link or scan the code below.

https://geni.us/GrumpBonusTL

Thank you so much for taking the time to read this book. If you enjoyed it, please let your friends know by leaving a review so more people can fall in love with Parker and Callum.

The one NIGHT stand before CHRISTMAS

The only thing worse than having a one-night stand with a ridiculously hot stranger during a snowstorm in Boston?

Finding out he's your ex-boyfriend's father.

In my defense, I didn't know the tall, broody man in the tailored suit would turn out to be Joshua's dad.

I also didn't expect him to spend Christmas in my quaint small town of Sycamore Falls.

Or attend every single one of the town's holiday events.

Or look at me like we're still back in that hotel room.

Now I'm currently one awkward sleigh ride away from a full-blown holiday meltdown. Because Declan Hart? He has bad idea written all over him.

Not only is he some hotshot attorney with a military past, but he has a voice as smooth as whiskey and a body that makes my tinsel curl.

He's also completely off-limits.

Which wouldn't be a problem…

If I could just stop thinking about that night.

Or how his eyes light up in the snow.

Or what might happen if we get caught under the mistletoe again.

This Christmas, I might be the one getting tangled up in something I really shouldn't want.

***The One Night Stand Before Christmas* is a small town, forbidden age gap holiday romance. Grab your copy today!**

MARRIED
to the
FRENEMY

It's the perfect plan.

He needs a wife in order to buy the vineyard where he's worked for years. I need a place to live with my four-year-old daughter.

All I have to do is pretend I'm madly in love with Beckham Lawrence, and I get to live rent-free for the next year.

There's just one problem.

Beckham hates me. I can't blame him. After all, I'm the reason he spent a year of his life behind bars.

The last thing I expect is for the tattooed grump to give my daughter the bedroom of her dreams.

Or to walk in on him reading her bedtime stories.

Or for him to sacrifice everything when her sperm donor makes a surprise appearance after all this time.

This was just supposed to be pretend.

But with every day, I start to imagine what it would be like for Beckham to call me his wife and mean it.

ACKNOWLEDGMENTS

Thank you so much for reading *The Grump Who Saved Christmas*.

I've been wanting to write small town romance for years.

For those of you new to me, I've been writing high heat billionaire romantic suspense since 2013 under the pen name, T.K. Leigh. (Although I have thrown a few lighter billionaire romances in there when I've needed a break from all the...well, murder.)

But as much as I love writing romantic suspense, I also love small town romance. Unfortunately, it's such a HUGE departure from my dark and gritty billionaire romances that I didn't feel it would be right to do those under my normal pen name.

So Tracy Leigh was born.

In the beginning of 2023, I said this would be the year I'd launch my small town pen name.

And I also said it would be the year I'd write a Christmas book.

And then it hit me. I could launch my small town pen name WITH a Christmas book.

So I redid some plans and made it an introduction to the world of Sycamore Falls. And I can't wait to share more of this world with you soon with Haley's story.

But first, I wanted to thank some people, all of whom jumped on board when I told them in September I'd be writing a Christmas book, while I was still in edits on my October release… Never a dull moment around here.

So, a huge thanks to my husband, Stan, and my daughter, Harper Leigh. Writing a book takes a lot of time and they've been my cheerleaders since day one. (Harper helped me choose the girl on the cover. So thanks, Harper!)

To my wonderful PA, Melissa Crump — thanks for always going along for the ride with all my crazy ideas. Like launching a small town pen name at the end of the year. LOL

To my fantastic beta readers — Lin, Melissa,, Stacy, and Vicky — thanks for always reading for me and offering feedback. And especially at the last minute.

To my admin team — Melissa and Vicky. Thanks for keeping my reader group and page running. Love you ladies!

To my review team — Thank you for always not only reading my books but also taking the time to write reviews, especially when I sprung this one on you all at the last minute. Surprise! LOL

To my reader group — Thanks for being my super-fans and giving me a place to go when I need a break from writing.

And last but not least, a big thank you to YOU! Thank you so much for picking up this book and taking a chance on it. Whether you've been a long-time T.K. Leigh reader or are just finding me now in this new genre, I'm so happy you took the time to read my words.

Can't wait to share even more stories with you very soon.

Love & Peace,
~ Tracy

ABOUT *the* AUTHOR

Tracy Leigh is the spicy small town alter ego of USA Today Bestselling author T.K. Leigh. She lives outside of Raleigh with her husband, daughter, special needs rescue dog, and three cats.

When she's not penning her next small town romance filled with heat and heart, she can be found reading, spending time with her family, or planning her next escape to Hawaii.

facebook.com/tracyleighbooks
instagram.com/tkleigh
tiktok.com/@tracyleighauthor
bookbub.com/authors/t-k-leigh
pinterest.com/tkleighauthor

www.ingramcontent.com/pod-product-compliance
Lightning Source LLC
Chambersburg PA
CBHW010549170726
48285CB00011B/2830